How did Joyce Stanger come to choose a wildcat as the chief character of her latest novel? One summer she and her family took their caravan to Scotland and with them their Siamese cat, normally an inquisitive, over-bold animal. They camped at a lonely site beside a loch. Unexpectedly the Siamese would not leave the caravan – he shivered at every sound and indeed some of the sounds, wails, and banshee screams were terrifying and at night sleep was impossible.

The author suspected wildcats were the cause and this was confirmed by the gamekeeper who had actually seen them. When Joyce Stranger left Scotland the memory of the wildcats continued to tantalise her, so she read everything she could find about them – questioned farmers, foresters, and gamekeepers for information on this mysterious cat. The result is a fascinating and vivid story of an animal whose courage and endurance first stimulated Joyce Stranger's curiosity and then gained her respect and admiration: feelings which will undoubtedly be shared by her readers.

Also by Joyce Stranger

and published by Corgi Books

Joyce Stranger

Chia, The Wildcat

CORGI BOOKS

CHIA, THE WILDCAT

A CORGI BOOK 0 552 09141 3

Originally published in Great Britain
by Harvill Press Limited

PRINTING HISTORY
Harvill Press edition published 1971
Corgi edition published 1973
Corgi edition reprinted 1975
Corgi edition reissued 1975
Corgi edition reprinted 1976
Corgi edition reprinted 1978
Corgi edition reissued 1983

This book is set in Georgian 10/10½ pt.

Corgi Books are published by Transworld Publishers Ltd.,
Century House, 61–63 Uxbridge Road,
Ealing, London, W5 5SA
Made and printed in Great Britain by
Hunt Barnard Printing Ltd., Aylesbury, Bucks.

To my mother and father,
with my love

Acknowledgements

My thanks are due to David Stephen and to
Dr J. Lochie of Edinburgh University, both of
whom very kindly helped me with information
on the habits of wildcats; very little indeed is
known about them as they are most elusive.
Much of this story is based on deduction rather
than fact, but every attempt has been made to
ensure that the animal lore is as accurate as
possible.

CHAPTER ONE

It was a declaration of war. Fergus McKenzie had no choice.

War from the day she came to his territory, just after dawn, arrowed into his yard, and stood bloody-mouthed, astounded when the keeper appeared at his window. The grouse, urgent in its death struggles, dangled from her jaws. Fergus, having heard the noise, flung up the bedroom window and shouted at her. The dogs barked. Startled, she dropped the bird and stood hissing at him, and then she was gone, fire-flash fast, leaping the wall and vanishing like smokehaze. Fergus was furious. The grouse had a nest in the heather beyond his garden, and she fed with his chickens. He had a liking for this particular bird. The grouse had an absurd and endearing character, regarding itself as a barnyard fowl, tame, and belonging to man. It often stood its ground and challenged the dogs, even defying Rob the sheepdog that herded every creature around the place capable of movement when the mood took him. The keeper dismissed his feeling with a half-grin, classing it, even to himself, as idiotic. He dressed and recovered the mauled carcase. It would feed the dogs.

Chia!

It was vituperative as a swear word, the sound the wildcat had made, and Fergus christened her with it. The beast would have to die.

The world narrowed temporarily to contain only the two of them. Narrowed to Chia's forays and Fergus's rage and the slain bodies of the birds she left to mock him, killing more than her need, eating only a part of each, although she could not know that this alone would madden him. She was swifter than the swooping hawk and twice as cunning

9

and Fergus was impatient. She raided ruthlessly, finding easy prey, dodging the man as she watched him and learned his habits.

He built a stronger run for his hens, and built pens for the ducks and geese that lived on the little tarn beyond the house. He could not stop the wanderers, and Chia caught them. She haunted the place, seldom seen, although her misdeeds bore eloquent witness to her presence. She met Bran, the Labrador pup, unexpectedly in the wood and, surprised by his sudden appearance, slashed his nose with a vicious raking paw. He turned on her, snarling and biting, but she fled to the trees and was gone, leaving Bran with a burning memory and a driving need to bark whenever he caught the tang of her, borne on the telltale breeze.

She watched from her secret places, two eyes in the bushes, knowing herself well hidden. She was waiting for time to pass. She had borne one litter already and knew what was to follow. She waited for the sons and daughters that would be hers. She was hungry and game was scarce. The man-place offered temptation and she changed her habits, sometimes hunting by day, her need to survive dominating her and overcoming her nocturnal nature. Long-legged, ringtail bushy, wide catface alert, swift to savagery, ears pricked, green eyes lambent, she was beautiful. Yet she was wicked, she was fierce, she was she-devil incarnate in muscled body and tawny tabby fur, and Fergus had only one desire left. To kill her.

He stalked her at midnight when her lonely cries assailed the distant stars. He crept behind her when she wandered at the edge of the loch, but the ground vibration told her he was there, even when he had read the wind and ensured that she did not catch the scent of him. She vanished into the undergrowth, and neither track nor trace did he find.

He stood at his window, in the dark, watching, pretending the house was deserted, sure she would come again to his chickens, or try her fury on Bran, or on Tim, the other Labrador, an older beast, wise with years and grey in muzzle. His Jack Russell terrier might attack her. Jack was too bold for his own good. Perhaps she would tangle with Dragon, his one-eyed ginger cat, who had been blinded, when he was only half grown, in a fight with a prowling fox. Dragon had been neutered long ago and was not interested in female cats. Fergus had no fear that perhaps his own cat might provide a mate. Rob was also a fighter, but Fergus checked him. It took too long to train a sheepdog and life would be impossible without Rob to herd the beasts.

Wildcats hated man and feared him. Fergus lived in isolation; as keeper, stalker, and shepherd, in sole charge of an estate suffering from modern economics, he spent many hours away from home, and Chia knew that the place was deserted when no dog barked at her stealthy approach. She had all the time in the world and she watched and learned that the chickens and ducks were released from the wooden huts before the man left the place. She waited, sprawled in a tree, her scent blown away on the vagrant wind.

She had the moor to herself as Fergus patrolled his boundaries. She heard him on his return, long before he reached his house, and was away to her secret strongholds, running swiftly through tracks she knew as well as she knew the strength of her vicious claws.

Fergus was sure that she would try for his ducks, or for the chicks that could crawl through the smallest space and escape his vigilance; or she might chase and catch Tip, the tame jackdaw that adored the keeper and followed him wherever he went. Fergus had found Tip trapped in the wire of the chicken run, trying to get his head through the mesh to steal the tempting grain. The run was roofed to foil the wildcat and Tip could not fly down and feed fat as he had done before her arrival.

Once she nearly caught him and snatched a tail feather, and Tip sounded his tocsin call, alarming all the birds in the bushes and the chickens and ducks and geese. He flew indoors through an open window to find sanctuary. Fergus, coming wearily home after a long stalk on the hill, was alerted by the din and raced towards the sound, his gun ready. Nothing was there but the noise that saluted Chia's invasion. He saw her shadow fly across the grass as she ran for the trees. His shot did not go near her.

He had lived in the wilderness for most of his life, many miles from his nearest neighbour, policing the land for the laird who owned it. He was a tall man, broad shouldered, yet slender and wiry, dark haired and big bearded, his face gaunt, his blue eyes fierce. He was a wary man, suspicious of strangers, as reluctant for company as the wildcat herself. He was dour, and used to living alone. He hated the hurry and bustle of towns and rarely drove to the village, where men regarded him with hostility and women with fear.

The children watched eagerly for him, seeing in him adventure and mystery, as he swung down the village street looking straight in front of him, his eyes aching for the far vistas over the moors, the gun in his hand as much a part of him as the jackdaw on his shoulder and the four dogs that followed closer than his shadow, at his heels. He had no need of other men, or women either, and no desire to waste precious hours in prattling small talk, or to exchange opinions in the bar at night. The village was too far from his home and he had other interests.

He loved to be alone on lochside or tarnside or by the deep pool in the burn, his fly floating on the water as he waited for a fish to take the delicately fragile lure, while the dippers curtseyed and throbbed as they filled the air with song.

He walked the hills by day and by night, observing the secret life that hid in bush and bracken; noting the alarm calls of birds that told him of fox or stoat or weasel; watching to ensure that rustlers did not come to steal his sheep or poachers to take his deer. He guarded his solitude, treasuring it. His life was filled from dawn to dusk. Not only the wildcat threatened him. He warred on rat and raiding fox and hungry eagle, respecting and admiring the wild beasts, but forced to kill those that turned to easy prey in his barnyard or among the lambs. He too had to ensure his livelihood. He lived alone in the stone house on the hill, drawing water from the well, tending the oil lamps, burying the household rubbish in pits he dug in the boggy ground beyond the tarn. He was hated by the men who came to poach on windless nights when the moon was only a memory, because, no matter how stealthily they crept, Fergus and his dogs usually found them.

He had friends, but they were men he saw rarely. They were men of his own kind, who flighted and gentled hawks, who bred and trained dogs, or who farmed in the wicked hills where death came wintrily with the sudden snow. He had a radio telephone in the house, linking him with the foresters who lived closer to the town and were connected by telephone.

His time was unbounded by clocks: it was measured by seasons, by dawn and sunset, by still days, and by wild days, when the wind screamed in fury; by deer that roved the valleys till the snow lay deep, and then sought the wind-swept crags where the snow could not lie. When the gales hurled abuse at the trees the beasts hid in shelters that only they knew. His days were dominated by small creatures that lived in a world of their own and travelled the beast walks and the wild ways, and he gained his wealth from that.

His wealth was knowledge. Knowledge of the badger's haunts and the deer's hiding grounds, and the nest made by a fieldmouse in the dry summer grass. Knowledge of the hawk's flight and the wind's might and the soar of the eagle. Money did not matter to him. It served to buy cartridges and a change of diet for himself and the beasts he owned. His gun brought most of their meat; his rod brought fish, and that he shared with Dragon, the old cat, who mostly killed for himself.

Fergus tilled his land, which was part of him, necessary to him as life. There was solace in the soil; in digging deep, in sowing and in reaping, and rich satisfaction that could not be gained in any other way. His chickens and his pigs and his plot of kitchen garden filled in the few hours that were spare. The deer management took much of his time, and there were daily chores with the sheep; chores that in the lambing season were endless.

The Highland cows gave him calves each year and he tended them when the weather was too wild to offer comfort, and the ground, on which they grazed, water-logged and starvation-poor. Kit and Kattie came to his call for titbits. Kit loved bread and apples and Kattie adored the winter turnips and crunched them noisily and messily. Sometimes her greed for them led her into pushing open the door of the store shed and eating until pain overtook her and Fergus had to cure her of the result of her folly. Kit and Kattie's calves went to swell the Laird's herd, to wander in the big park some miles away. Shaggy-haired, with upswept horns, they eyed the world of men and cars and tractors with uncomplaining and uncomprehending wonder.

The dogs were Fergus's company and shared his home, and he asked for nothing more.

The wildcat had not been born on Fergus's territory. She had come there for safety, away from the traps and guns in the place where she had been bred. The tom that mated her, brief and exultant, on an icy March night, calling his triumph under a cold full moon, was the first of several wildcats that died, and hung by their paws from the wire fence beside the stiff bodies of moles and weasels and carrion crows.

Long after she had forgotten her mate, Chia bore him a litter. She fed the kittens, rapturous in motherhood, but she was young and not yet wily. As they grew, one fell victim to a hunting stoat; a second to a questing owl; the third, venturing out alone, was trapped in the bog and drowned. The last kitten was caught in the snare that had caused his father's death.

Chia watched the kitten die over a spell of days, held by his throat in a wire noose that cut but did not kill at once, and that tightened as he struggled. She tore her own jaws trying to bite away the strangling wire; she brought him food that he could not eat and licked his weakening body, lying close against him, offering the only comfort she knew. When he was almost dead, and breath a faint flicker in his throat, and his dull eyes saw nothing, she drove away the stoats that came to feed, but at least he died and Chia left him. The stoats and the carrion crows had their way. She recognised death. The kitten was lost for ever. She abandoned her home place and sought safer quarters, high on the rocky hill, in a lair made by a tumble of fallen rock.

She lived alone all summer, and when snow lay on the ground and March once more unseasonably enthralled the lochs and bound them in ice, she met a roving tom and ran with him for a week. They were on remote farmland, tempted by the hens, and the farmer, a patient man, baited a trap with a newly dead bird and hid. The tom rolled and stretched to the sharp knell of the gun, and Chia, who had been hiding, crept away, making herself small and thin, belly against the ground, ears flat on her head, legs crouched. She trembled with terror. She had never heard guns before, nor seen the instant death that followed their noise. When the moon swung up the sky that night and shone carefree on loch and moor and mountain, she ran for sanctuary, looking for a place where bushes grew thick and cover was plentiful and man did not bide.

She hunted as she went; small mice died and small birds fluttered in her jaws and were swiftly killed, and a fox scented her and circled, wary, knowing her too much for him. He had once, when he was a half-grown cub and not yet wise, fought with a wildcat and his muzzle was scored by the deep raking claws and one eye was scarred, so that he was nicknamed, by men who saw him, Old Scarface. Chia spat at him, and he loped hastily by, anxious to leave her all the space in the world.

She was restless and uneasy. She was lonely for her own kind and for the quick matings under the moon and the yells and screams and fights with other cats. She lay in dense heather, and drank from the pools in the rocks and learned to avoid the bogs, and eased herself with fresh green grass when her belly felt too full, and she waited.

The second time Fergus saw her clearly she had come close to his home and found a plump duck wandering on its own, and run off with it dangling from her jaws, quacking its panic for all the other birds to mimic, so that the yard was senseless with noise and horrid with fear. He was walking back from the sheep hill, too far away to risk a shot. Irritation mounted rapidly to fury at her impudence. She sped over the wall and through the long pathway under the brambles, the duck hampering her, wings thrashing in terror. She climbed a fallen tree, sloped against other trees so that the trunk was inclined, the roots still growing in the earth, the feather-soft spring haze of opening leaves rustling on the sap-filled branches. Here she killed and ate her catch, hidden in shade and sheltered from view, the dapple of light blending her tabby coat with the mottled sun-flecked tree trunk. On the ground, next day, Fergus found the telltale feathers and marked yet another place where he might find her.

Chia watched him from above, hidden, eyes narrowed. The dogs were hunting rabbit and did not sense her. Man-scent was foul on the air. When Fergus had gone she sharpened her claws, scoring the tree, and washed her fur, licking industriously, cleaning away the blood from her last meal, before climbing the hill to the tiny cave above the stream that was now her lair.

The cave was small, a shelter formed by three large rocks that leaned together. Space enough for a cat, with a sandy floor that she hollowed slightly and filled with tangled grass and leaves. It was dry, and soft for sleep, though sleep was wary, alert, one eye half open for danger; never deep and relaxed, like a domestic creature. The three exits made the cave a good place, offering her a choice should she need to flee.

As the days passed her body thickened. She was slower, and unwilling to clamber into the trees. Spring came with a flourish of blossom, with white wind-flowers, bluebells, and new shoots on the heather, with the yellow-green acid-sharp bogmoss. There were young foxes in the den beyond the bend in the burn, and owlets and eaglets on the nests and every creature had a mate and she had none.

She lay at the mouth of the cave, sprawled, half asleep in the spring sunshine, her tabby fur splendid and gleaming, day after day moving only when evening spilled its shade. She found rabbit and leveret and mouse, and once a shrew, which she ate in desperation, raging with hunger, and which tasted evil so that her stomach rejected it. Her mother would have told her that shrews were protected by a small gland which tainted their flesh, but her mother had died too soon and Chia had to learn by experiment. It was not easy, but she was clever and agile and strong and she learned fast and never repeated a single mistake. Mistakes in the wilderness could rarely be remedied. Death came swiftly to those who erred, however briefly.

Fergus, watching for her daily, found only the scats that she left foxlike on the ground, denoting that she was true wildcat and not tame cat gone feral. Dragon, his own cat, was aware of her but had fortunately not been out of doors when she came, or there might have been a battle that scarred both beasts, for none should invade his territory.

Fergus hoped that her scats might betray her if she left them near her home, but she emptied herself far from her lair, aware of the need for cleanliness and caution, and he found neither track nor trace nor clue to her hiding place.

She approached through water and over rock and, even when heavy with young, she jumped the last stretch and left no mark, landing on slippery granite. She hid by day and wandered at night and cried to the ghost of the moon. She was lonely and needed company. She called, but only Dragon heard her; he bristled his ruff and fluffed his tail and swore at the gathering dark.

The days passed. Chia wandered less. The growing, struggling kits hampered her breathing. Movement was difficult, and she was weary, and glad to sleep for the greater part of both day and night. It was not easy to catch her food. She was slow, her balance uncertain, her pounce mistimed and her paws less agile. Fergus glimpsed her briefly one night, in the distance, outlined by the glim of the moon, and saw that she was to give birth very soon. He swore. He drove fifty miles to the town for more cartridges and cleaned his gun and haunted the place where he had seen her, but she was far too clever for him.

The sun of late April dived over the peaks and darkness swallowed the day, and the night was wicked and wild with wind, and the mountains called their hatred and thunder echoed and rolled. Chia shuddered and listened and paced her lair, desperate with pain. Pain that knifed and needled, that made her gasp and wail, and tore her body apart.

She scratched frantically at the ground, digging and clawing, seeking to ease the monstrous agony that devoured her, blinding her to the world outside. A massive thrust sent the first kit tumbling from beneath her tail. This brought momentary relief, and she looked down at the tiny thing that lay on the ground, apparently lifeless. It moved, a feeble twitch of one paw. Memory flooded her brain, so that she recalled her other kittens and bent at once to lick the tiny body, to massage it with her tongue, to encourage it to life.

Pain distracted her once more. A second kit followed the first. A third, a fourth, and then a fifth. The pain eased and she dropped to the ground exhausted, panting, her breath sucking the air in harrowing gasps. The night was ending and the thin promise of dawn greyed the air outside, and the chill wind of the hills filtered into the cave and fingered her fur.

She left the cave, dragging herself to the nearby burn's edge, only two yards away, avid for water. A final pain savaged her and the afterbirth came from her. She sniffed it, and instinct told her to eat, to remove every trace, so that no predator could track her down, or smell the blood. When the last scrap was gone she scratched the ground, burying the scent, obliterating it with the smell of fresh-turned earth, strong on the air.

She drank thirstily, greedily, every drop savoured, her busy tongue lapping till she could hold no more. Her ears listened, and between laps she lifted her head and sniffed the wind, which told her of a deer below her, offering no danger, and brought news of birds in the brush, and also brought a sharp tang from the seawrack that coloured the edge of the distant loch and dried on the shore.

She paused, looking round her, hidden by the dense shrubby undergrowth that bordered the banks of the burn. She had not been sighted by any other creature. All was still except for the rush of water over the boulders. There was only the cheep of quietly busy birds, unalarmed, about their own affairs. There was only the shadow of the soaring sparrowhawk, flying over the ground, intent on other business than hers. He swooped and one mouse less rustled in the grass. He flew to his nest.

Chia watched, one paw lifted, eyes narrowed, ears alert. There was a sound, a hint of a whisper, a faint murmur on the air. She looked towards the cave, and cocked her head, ears pointed to catch the noise, eyes wide. The sound came again, stronger, a pathetic mewling whimper, the desperate cry of a tiny beast, cold and alone, alive in a cruel world. She ran towards the cave, forgetting her wet pawmarks on the ground, failing to jump the last few steps and flashed into the lair.

The five slimed bundles were moving. A soft, minute paw touched her leg, a delicate tap, a feather-breath and she was intensely aware of them, of the scent of them, of the feel and the taste and the softness of them, knowing they were hers, were part of her, torn from her, hers to cover and caress, hers to feed and teach. The ferocity of possession was so intense that, in the driving passion of love, her busy licking tongue almost savaged them, the thread, between adoration and killing them and eating them in warped blind eagerness, drawn thin. Only the movement of one of them against her swollen teats brought sense back to her. The birth had been difficult and she was not yet mistress of her emotions.

She settled herself and suckled them. Her racing heart slowed and the excitement that mastered her faded to pride. She licked the blind heads tenderly, savouring the tiny beasts that birth had released from the imprisonment of her body. They sought for food and love and she had both for them. She curled herself around them, each one pushing against her. Her eyes were half-closed in ecstasy, as she surveyed each kit with delight. Her throaty purr of exultant motherhood was loud enough to alert Bran as he walked with his master on the other side of the burn.

The Labrador stopped and cocked his head, listening. The sun sleeked his black coat, and he glanced back at Fergus, who stiffened to attention, and then shook a cautionary finger as he caught the sound. He was without his gun, having come to fish in the early dawn, to try for a trout before the sun warmed the water, to see what was astir in the greylit woods and to look over the deer herd that sheltered in the far corrie and watch for new calves. The Jack Russell was sniffing eagerly, longing for foxes. He watched Fergus, bright eyes hopeful, head cocked on one side. Rob sat, obedient.

Tim, too, was testing the air, his wise eyes watchful. He caught the unmistakable cat tang and growled breathily. Fergus glanced across the burn. The pawmarks were not yet dry. He knew the cave. A vixen had borne cubs there five years before. He knew the site well. He had killed her first litter. She found a better site next year. He only discovered that when the cubs were grown.

'Stay,' he said and the dogs sat, patient, and watched their master cross the water and vanish among the trees.

Chia smelled him. She heard the footsteps on the rock, felt the vibrating telltale from the man's weight on the ground, felt it with all her body, stretched flat, sheltering her young. Her savage hiss, as he came towards the cave, caught the keeper off guard and he jumped back, knowing that she had given birth, and knowing, too, that, if he persisted in trying to see, her claws would rip his face and she might blind him. No sane man ever challenged a wildcat, with kits, walled up in her den. It was the only time she would attack man. At all other times she would flee. He would return to the house and bring his gun and entice her with the bloody entrails of the blue hare he had shot the night before. She would be starving after giving birth, as she would not have left the cave on their first day of life to go hunting.

No wildcat was rearing a family on his territory. She would come for chicken and duck, greedy for herself and the growing young that would need more and more fresh killed meat as the days went by. She would, in her anxiety for them, respect no man's property. She would be doubly fierce, and when the kits grew there would be four or five of them on his ground, and her sons would mate her and mate their sisters, and the beasts would breed and bring destruction to his territory.

It was unthinkable.

CHAPTER TWO

Chia watched him go, terror racing her thudding heart. She was at his mercy and she was weak from birth. He would be back, she knew. She had to move the kits to a safer place, where he could not find them.

She did not want to leave them. Anything might happen in her absence. Experience told her that they were small and helpless and easy prey for fox and stoat and weasel and hunting hawk or crow. She had lost all her first litter long before they were grown.

She lifted one gently, her eldest, the heaviest, the first-born, a tiny tom that mewed as he felt her mouth close above him. He shifted his blind head, seeking her teat, and the warm milk that filled him and comforted him. She cherished the small weight hanging from her jaws but urgency mastered her and she dared not linger. She ran outside, where a fading sun had risen briefly and was dying, chased by shadowy clouds building in streaks, forecasting windrush, and she eyed the hill.

It was a foothill, lying at the edge of mountains, covered in bramble and brush and heather, a few sparse pines straggling in undergrowth that choked them. The burn slid across its rocky flank, where the earth was thin and sandy. Here, near her home, was only a meagre trickle over lichened rocks, but it should mask her scent. She trod in the water, slipping on the slime, carrying the kit carefully, his brief weight a feather burden. She laid him in the nesty hollow of an old tree, where thick leaves, blown from the autumnal rending, made a dense bed. He was totally helpless and could not stray, and she left him, trusting his safety to the bramble through which she had pushed her way and which hid the entrance to her refuge. Fear walked beside her, haunting her footsteps. She was torn by the desire to hurry, warring with the need for caution. She paused frequently, to listen and to test the wind.

She went back again and again, struggling against exhaustion, hunger riding her, uncomfortable with the milk that filled her, until at last five kits were bedded in the leaves, their small paws reaching towards her, their heads seeking food. She lay suckling them, every muscle tense, as she listened for the sound of boots thumping the ground and the terrifying pad, pad, pad of the dogs' heavy tread. The man would bring both Labradors, she knew. She had learned much of his ways from her secret eyries in the preceding weeks.

When the kits were fed and sleeping, small bodies curled warmly one against another, she left them and climbed the tree, lying along the branch, watching for danger. She heard the man return and she waited, ears flattened, hissing softly, swearing under her breath. She was high above the deserted cave, but could see it plainly.

Fergus approached the lair carefully, his gun ready. He did not want the dogs to tangle with the wildcat. He saw the mazed pattern of paw prints where she had crossed and re-crossed her own tracks. He wondered if some other intruder had come and done his work for him. There was complete silence. No soft rustle, no hint of movement. No warning hiss. He knew she had gone.

He bent to look beneath the rocks. The place was bare, except for blood that stained the stones, the tangled grasses of her nest, and a heap of feathers blowing in a wind that was strengthening to a gale. Wind mourned in the heather and whined along the burn and teased at the trees. Fergus put his hand down and felt the bed. The ground was cold. He looked at the paw marks, and knew that, once more, she had eluded him. He set the dogs on the scent.

Bran, too young to know his job, found the smell of rabbit and chased it gaily, drank noisily from the burn and came back to stand by Fergus, his tail waving. He hated being alone. Tim followed the cat scent to the burn, hunted along the bank, and was baffled. Jackie quartered the ground busily before he too gave up and wagged an uncertain tail. Fergus sat on a rock and stared at the water. The cat had defeated him again. Bran was beside him, pawing at his leg, wanting attention, hating to be ignored. Tim, older and more patient, dropped to the ground, but did not take his eyes away from his master, knowing that soon there would be a signal that he must obey. Jackie opened his mouth in a grin. He was a merry little dog.

Above them, the eagle circled, aware of the man and the dogs. He glimpsed the wildcat sprawled along a branch. He had not seen her carry her kits. He needed food for his mate, busy incubating her two eggs, which were close to hatching. The bird was twelve years old and wise with experience, knowing that many beasts had young at this time of year. He marked the wildcat's hiding place.

High above him the wind whistled the cloud packs and hunted across the sky.

Fergus sat still, noting the half-hidden, velvet covered, new growing knobs of a browsing stag, only its head apparent among the thinly covered new-leafed bushes: knowing that a fieldmouse crouched terrified, brilliant-eyed, panting in alarm, not five feet away from his booted foot, watched with interest by Tim and Jackie, who both knew better than to get up and investigate. Bran sat and stood and lay down, and then stood again, impatient. Fergus would not tolerate the dogs hunting. Bran would never run off alone. His eagerness for activity warred with his Labrador instinct for obedience, but instinct for training won. He was totally man's dog, never his own master.

Fergus patrolled till the sun vanished from the sky. He waited until the moon rode high and the wind screamed in the trees before he slept, but sleep he must. The night was quiet. Chia was hunting mice close to her home. She was not yet ready to leave the kittens for any length of time. Fergus relaxed his watch as the nights passed without incident.

Four nights later the wind was blowing even more strongly. The wildcat left her young and watched until the house was dark. She was hidden, secret, guarding her scent, silent as snowfall, so that the dogs did not see her, did not smell her, and the keen of the wind hid the outcry in the duckpen, which she broached with a wicked paw that tugged the wire from the staples that held it. She left her memory in the yard, among the spilled blood and tossing feathers, taking the duck that she killed with her, back to her lair on the hill. It was quicker to take a duck than to hunt for rabbit. She was exceedingly hungry and mice did not fill her, and she did not wish to leave her young alone for too long.

Fergus, waking early, went to feed the barnyard creatures and stared in incredulous fury at the heaped white feathers that lay in the yard. Beyond them, insolently pointing her scorn, was the wildcat's trademark. The dogs sniffed at it in blank amazement.

Not one, but five ducks were gone. Fergus saw the blood trail that led to the bramble path. He was sure that she must have spent the night killing in his duckpen, feeding fat so that she could rear her young. Her action honed his anger, inducing him to find his gun, and follow the trail. But Chia had been too clever. She had taken to the trees, and the dogs could not track her.

The wildcat had killed one duck only. She carried her victim away. A passing vixen caught the scent and came and slaughtered. The ducks were free, unattended, having slipped, panic stricken, through the wire, trying to escape death. The urge to kill was paramount, so that when one was dead she turned to another, and yet another, until four lay on the ground. The remainder fled, and flew into the trees.

The vixen carried the first up the hill. Her den was closer than the wildcat's lair. She had only time to take two of the birds before the dog fox that had mated her, and now was hunting on his own, came by and took the third. The vixen was feeding five cubs. She ate part of one duck and buried the remains and the second carcase, a provident store for the morrow, when her hunting might go unrewarded.

Dragon had been sleeping in the shelter of a bush, as the night was warm and he did not wish to lie indoors. He ranged the hill when darkness invaded the sky, and was away from home when cat and foxes came by. He returned and found a dead duck in the yard. Food in plenty. Fergus expected the cat to hunt for himself, and he fed fat on rat and mouse, but duck was luxury. Dragon seized the trophy and fled, as far away as possible. Fergus never knew that his own cat had eaten the vixen's kill, nor that the wildcat was unjustly blamed for the carnage.

Chia, now safe and far away, crouched over her catch, tore at the flesh and packed her belly. She was hungrier than she had ever been in her life. Her first litter had been small, had not lived long, and had made slight demands on her. These kits were large and healthy and their appetites were already voracious. She could not leave them long. She ran to the hollow and crept in among the leaves and the five heads turned to her instantly, scenting the rich milk, and the kits rolled over one another, pushing and struggling in their efforts to find the teats and suck. They were much stronger than they had been four days ago.

Chia licked them, and when they had fed, her warm tongue massaged each small belly beneath the tail, stimulating nature to her work. Without her action the kittens would retain their water and die. She knew, without teaching, what she must do.

When they curled to sleep she tucked herself round them, her body relaxed and warm, sheltering them from the sneak of wind and the slash of rain that filtered in through the hole. High in the branches above them a red squirrel had her drey. Her own young were not yet born. A stray breeze brought a whiff of the wildcat to her, and she left at once, to find another place in which to give birth. There was no safety here. Should the wildcat climb the tree she would find the nest and raid it. The squirrel was soon busy restoring an abandoned nest and lining it with moss and tangled moulted fur, left along the deer fences from beasts that scratched away the irritating winter moult. She had a rich source of bedding.

Chia slept all day. The kits woke and fed and slept and woke again. That night she left the tree just before dusk, and the birds called a warning. Chatter of chaffinch and blackbird and starling alerted the hill and anger stalked before her, and small beasts, hidden in the undergrowth, scurried to hide, or froze, feigning death.

Chia crept into cover. Every time she walked abroad the birds heralded her coming. The sharp angry notes sounded behind her and in front of her. Rabbits heard the tocsin and thumped, stamping on the ground and fleeing, white

25

scuts bobbing, and the grazing deer vanished, to stand in the shadows, not a muscle moving. They were terrified by the wildcat scent, and by the size of her. Her glossy fur was thick upon her, her black and tawny tail erect, her yellow-green eyes narrowed and devilish. Tiger markings showed clearly on her head.

Murder has come, the birdnotes called, as Chia stalked among them. She was slim again and no longer slowed by the weight of her kits. An unwary chaffinch fluttered in front of her and she leaped and slashed him out of the air. He died as he hit the ground, and she crouched and fed, ignoring the wails and cries that surrounded her and that alerted Fergus, walking on the far side of the hill, returning from a day among the sheep. He whistled under his breath, to call the dogs to heel, but he knew she would hear him. No matter how lightly he trod she sensed the thud in the ground, and his scent and that of the dogs was strong on the air.

She fled towards home, bounding over the burn. She could not elude the bird calls, but she could run faster than the man tracking her and was soon safe, racing towards the tree. A stoat met her in the half-light, hissed, and swiftly vanished. Dusk was deepening to dark. The moon, playing with the flying clouds, shone and hid, and a tawny owl called, lonely, in the night. There was no sound, no hint, no flicker of tail or flash of light on fur, no moving ear, no glowing green eyes. It was going to be a long and patient vigil, all summer long, but Fergus had sworn to himself that the wildcat would die and die she must.

The dogs plodded behind him, patient. Bran longed for his bed. He hated night patrols, being a lazy dog, needing goading to come out when the hills were dark and the wind was fierce and the men who knew the deer haunts came to hunt, with no telltale moon to show their presence. Tim loved work and greeted Fergus eagerly when called to his duty. No one walked unchallenged on Tim's ground or dared to threaten his master. Bran was very young and might run in nervous fear, but Tim was staunch. A pat on the head and a pull of his ears was all he asked, while Bran needed a fuss and constant reassurance, especially when the wind whipped a branch with a snap and a scurry of leaves, or a strange noise startled the listening air. The Jack Russell was always eager, delighting in any activity that allowed him the company of his master. The Labradors were both well-loved, but Jackie and the keeper shared an extra bond, so that between them was total understanding.

Fergus patrolled the hill for an hour and then eased himself into the shelter of a huge old tree, leaning against the trunk, wishing he could smoke, but tobacco would betray him. The Labradors sprawled, nose on paws, and Bran dozed, but Tim remained alert and Jackie nosed his master's leg affectionately. Fergus pulled the terrier's ear in gentle acknowledgement.

It was eerie in the darkness. Fergus heard the skittering paws of a mouse as she scurried through the grass; knew that the badger had come from her earth and was scratching herself vigorously. Her leg thumped the ground. The dogs watched, Bran now wakeful, his nose telling him of the badger's presence. Jackie scented badger and his body trembled with excitement. Fergus touched the terrier, his hand pressing against the animal's back bidding him to be still. The dog knew better than to move. Fergus waited, but it was too dark to see. Badgers had always lived on the hill, liking the sandy soil that was well drained and dry and easy to dig. There were several earths nearby. There were probably cubs. The badgers rarely troubled him. Their food supplies lay elsewhere.

The clouds slid away from the moon. Light shone on the ground, and Fergus saw a flicker of movement, a telltale that showed him a stag sheltering beneath a tree, merged with the shadows. A moving ear betrayed the beast. A vixen ran lightly down the path. She was heavy with milk, betraying her motherhood. The keeper frowned. She was too close to his home and she too would be hunting.

There was no sign of the wildcat. Wherever she was hidden, he would have to find her. Another man might have set a snare, but snares were against Fergus's conscience. They killed too cruelly and he was a humane man. He shot to kill, or he did not risk a shot. A gun was quick and clean. A snare was devil's ploy, and he could not bear to find a beast dying after days of agony, when poachers set nooses for the hares.

Chilliness sneaked out of the night. Bran was cold and whimpered his annoyance. Reluctantly, Fergus turned for home. A dog fox, intent on his own business, saw the man and the dogs and froze in the bushes. Tim smelled the beast and his ruff bristled and he growled, but Fergus quieted him. Jackie was frantic but knew he must not run off. Foxes had been few on the hill the year before. They preyed on rat and rabbit. The keeper disliked killing them, but he sometimes had no choice. The eagle was clever, and fox cubs made a useful addition to his diet. Perhaps the bird would solve his problem and also take the wildcat's kits and, her litter gone, she would leave his territory to find a mate.

If she went for his lambs ... A new worry took the place of the old, and he picked his way through the night, stopping to listen for sound of car or of man, or a death scream that might tell him where the wildcat was hunting.

He heard nothing till he reached home. There was a thump and a sudden squeak. For one horrid moment he thought Chia had spent the night raiding his yard. He sighed with relief when Dragon came running towards him as he opened the door of the house and switched on his torch to give himself enough light to get a match to the oil lamp. The cat held a newly dead rat in his jaws and showed it proudly. Fergus complimented the animal gravely and put him outside again, and pondered the enigma of all cats and the quick baffling change from gentleness to ferocity in even the tamest hearthside puss. Dragon looked incapable of inflicting damage on any creature.

Tip greeted him ecstatically. The jackdaw was shut indoors at night and resented the imprisonment. Fergus could not risk the bird's eager noise as the bird watched the life around him and shouted an angry warning when stoat or fox were near. He would alert the wildcat. Fergus gave the bird three raisins, to console him for his lonely vigil. Tip ate greedily and settled on the back of the armchair, head cocked on one side, bright eyes inquisitive. The dogs curled on the hearthrug, close pressed for company, Tim with his head stretched on his paws, while Bran leaned his own head over the older dog's shoulder. Jackie lay with nose on his master's discarded shoe. Fergus looked at them and sighed.

Bed was not for him. He put the lamp on the table and took his notebooks and the map he had made of the estate, and marked the place where he thought the wildcat hid, and also where he had seen the vixen. Chia, knowing the man had gone and she herself was safe, went roaming and killed a young rabbit, and ate and drank and returned to her home and slept.

The kits were growing fast. They were almost one week old.

CHAPTER THREE

Motherhood sharpened Chia's wits. She was as elusive as a dream and scarcely more tangible. The keeper was forced to forget her. On the day that the kittens were one week old, the last day in April, the first lamb was born. Chia had a respite. Fergus was soon intolerably busy.

He quartered the hill by day and by night, wishing for the old days, when two keepers worked on the estate and a shepherd cared for the sheep. The estate was almost a sanctuary, as only the laird now shot the deer, helping Fergus with the annual cull that removed the sick and the weak, and prevented misery.

Sometimes a party met and guns were taken to the grouse, but the sheep were the mainstay of the place and Fergus's work lay with them. Lambing was late. Winter lasted long in that part of the country.

He would be busy for weeks, bringing home the lambing ewes. There were always casualties among them, and he had four orphans to bottle-feed, and a variety of odd tasks. He had made lambing pens near the house and most of the ewes were sheltered, but there was always some wily beast that avoided him and the dogs and hid herself; it was always she that had difficulty at birth.

There were birth cords to cut and disinfect, or there would be navel ill or joint ill. Ears needed notching, to brand the beasts lest they stray. Fergus no longer relied on the notch alone and each ewe and each new lamb wore an ear tag, bearing a number that made identification easy. The lambs had to be injected against lamb dysentery and pulpy kidney. Some of them did not know how to feed, and long hours were spent in patient guidance before the suckling habit was established.

Fergus was bone weary. He needed help. He had not enough time for half the jobs, and he could do no more than shoot in the air to discourage the eagle, or loose off at a marauding fox. He would have to find the vixen. He saw her several times in the distance, her wary head watching him. He saw nothing of Chia. He relied on the dogs to chase intruders. Tip, the jackdaw, gave good warning, and so did the Jack Russell. Even so the fox found a new-born lamb, one of twins, that had been neglected by the mother, who had evaded Fergus and was not found until one lamb was dead and the other starving, because it would not suck. The keeper cursed the fox, and the weather.

Spring was tardy. The air was wet and chill, and the new-born, rain-damp lambs had to be dried by the fire. The ewes were excited, awkward and unpredictable. Life was frustration, irritation and exhaustion, sleep, hastily snatched and never sufficient. The beasts became a symbol of slavery; hourlong, daylong, nightlong; care without respite. Fergus's eyes ached as he took hay to the penned ewes; his hands were reluctant to show their skill as he bent to the tiny beasts' cords; the water that sterilised the syringes was an age boiling, and the needles had minds of their own and blocked, or the plunger failed to work.

A week after lambing had started Fergus was busy with a ewe that had just lambed. As he left her he glanced at the rough road that bisected the hill. Headlights briefly slashed the night. No one had a right on the estate, and intruders had come, come almost certainly knowing that this was the worst time of his year, when he was stretched beyond endurance with the jobs among the sheep. He whistled the dogs and fetched his gun.

The night was still. The headlights had been on the far road. Fergus looked at his Land-Rover. It was tempting to use but its noisy engine would warn the men. He needed to hurry. He needed silence. He followed the steep path through the trees, trusting his eyes to show him pitfall and heather tump. The dogs, close behind him, were three stealthy shadows, knowing that here was work. Fergus was gripped by fury, as the hill seethed with hinds in calf.

Once the keeper stumbled and caught his foot in a hole that led, under a tree root, to a deep den where a fox sheltered. The fox was out, hunting. Fergus fell, heavily, shaking the breath from his body, and the thump drove a herd of hinds towards the hilltop and saved them from the poachers. Luckily the men heard nothing. Chia was hunting too. Prey was scarce, and she had twice missed a young rabbit, which dodged hastily into his burrow and lay quiet, recovering from fright. She was no longer merely hungry. She was ravenous, and driven to incaution in her need for food. She heard the men and slipped into cover, but she knew the deer were near, and the noise and smell of them roused her to savagery. She stalked warily, ears flattened, nose never still as she questioned the grass and listened to the wind, seeking news of passing beasts that might fill her and quieten the intense ache within her.

The three men had left their van and were fanned out in the shelter of trees planted by the foresters. Two hinds were outlined in the moonlight that brightened a little rocky glen beyond them. Neither was alarmed.

Two guns spoke together. Fergus, creeping towards the men, led by the dogs, who relied on their noses, stopped to listen. The panic bleat and thump of feet told him that one deer at least had been hurt, but not killed. She was running into a corrie that slanted across the hill and the men were chasing after her, no longer wary, sure that the keeper was lying in his bed, exhausted by his work on the sheep hill.

Fergus waited. Deer and men were coming towards him and he had the advantage of surprise. The hind, her neck torn open by a spreading bullet, was hurting cruelly and bleeding profusely. Her one desire was to run, to run away from harm and to evade the men who pounded after her.

She turned aside and ran into a hollow backed by a steep wall of rock. She could go no further. She dropped, exhausted, and Chia, who had been running alongside her, hidden, avidly aware of the smell of blood, raced in, attacking viciously and the hind died, mercifully, as her injury was appalling. The poachers, far behind, traced the blood trail.

They paused at the entrance to the hollow. It was narrow, the remains of an old quarry, long forgotten and long unworked. The moon shone on the dead hind. The shot had missed the second deer and she was safely away on the hill, hidden, panting after her escape. Chia looked up in alarm. She had forgotten caution in her hunger.

'Bloody cat!' one of the men said in disgust.

Chia lifted her head. Hatred shone from her eyes; she flattened her ears and backed away. She was trapped, with only the rocky wall behind her.

'My God! It's a wildcat,' one of the men said. A domestic tabby might have been a simpler problem.

He lifted his gun, but he was slow and clumsy, not being an experienced marksman. Chia was terrified. She had to escape. Before the poacher could fire she sprang, not at him, but at the gap between him and the next man, at the open space that led to safety, that led away from disaster, that led to her lair and the waiting kittens.

The man, startled, fired and missed. The bullet slapped off the rock, the sound savaging the night. Fergus, above the intruders, saw their outlines black against the open ground. He saw Chia streak for safety, racing among the trees, as if aware that by use of the protection of their massed trunks she could escape the penalty of the gun. A second later she was gone, merged into the darkness, a memory on the air, a memory that made Jackie growl under his breath. Fergus flicked a finger and the dog was still.

The men turned to one another. Fergus, watching them, knew they were amateurs, looking for easy money. An experienced poacher would not have missed his beast, nor hesitated when faced with the wildcat. Chia had already mauled the deer, having had ten minutes before they came upon her. They were sure the wildcat had intended to attack them and the story would grow with time. They were unaware that she would never have dared, that her one desire was escape, away from the sight and sound and smell of them, away to dense cover that would hide her and enable her to regain her equanimity after her fright.

The men hesitated. The dead deer lay beyond them, and one of them walked towards it to see if he might salvage at least some of the beast. The towns paid well for venison. Fergus spoke from the trees.

'Drop your guns. You're covered.'

He loosed a bullet over their heads to reinforce his words.

Startled, they turned and stared, but could not see him. He was huddled close against a tree trunk, his dark clothes merging with the shadows, his face hidden by his beard. The three guns dropped to the ground. A second bullet was fired in the air.

'Now move away from them.' The disembodied voice dominated the poachers.

The men took several paces away from the guns, their faces hostile. When the weapons were out of reach Fergus loosed the dogs, and at once each animal ran and took up station near his own quarry. Jackie, aware of his small size compared with that of the man he was guarding, bared his teeth, and growled viciously. Rob circled, herding men and dogs alike, his eyes watchful. He was ready and eager, hoping for a chance to run in and bite. His mouth grinned mischievously. He knew that here was legitimate prey.

One of the men moved, raising his foot to kick Jackie.

'Don't let him fool you,' Fergus said grimly. 'He's more vicious than the other two put together. He can kill a fox on his own, and has done.' His quiet voice held authority.

There was no further argument. The men were herded up the hill towards the house. The gun and the dogs allowed them no choice. Inside, sitting together, the snarling dogs guarding them, they watched sullenly as Fergus sent out a call on the radio telephone. Movement was dangerous. The Labradors and the Jack Russell were unrelenting guards. Not for the first time, Fergus blessed civilisation which let him live as he chose, in isolation, yet gave him contact for emergencies. The forester promised to come and help with the prisoners. It was a short trip in his Land-Rover. Together they would drive to the village and hand over the men.

By this time the kittens had opened their eyes and Chia knew them well. The smallest, a little tom, was also the fiercest, and his quick hiss and snarl greeted any strange noise long before he could see.

The second tom was larger and lazier, except when he was hungry. Then he shouldered and pushed and butted, and tried to bite his sisters as he struggled to get most milk. His brother was more cunning and knew how to wait his time and grab fast, ousting another of the litter.

34

The three females were all of a size. The first was gentle, anxious for love, needing her mother's tongue on her head before she settled to feed, eager to greet Chia before the others; the second was curious, alert for every sound, her ears listening constantly to birdcall and wind song and the thrill of running water. The third wanted nothing from the world but the infinite satisfaction of food.

The wildcat explored the hill above her den. It was new territory to her, rising steeply from the loch, its lower slopes thickly covered in dense undergrowth. Trees, thrusting from the tangle, growing close and spindly, choked one another in their struggle for light. The burn ran close by her lair and, a few yards away, widened and swelled to a small river that foamed and frothed over tumbled boulders, to plunge headlong over a seven foot drop, where water cascaded down to a deep, swirling pool. Much of Chia's time was spent in a dense mat of jungley growth which blocked her view. Hidden, secret, she needed her ears and her nose, as her eyes could not see beyond her immediate surroundings.

Above the waterfall was a fallen tree, that spanned the burn and gave access to moorland, where hunting was easier than in the dense undergrowth and many small creatures hid.

Chia, roaming in the first light of an early May dawn, found a nest made of dry grass, cunningly woven into a hollow ball. She parted the strands with her paw and took the five blind baby mice that lay inside. The mother, returning later to her despoiled home, smelled the cat and mourned bitterly for three days, the milk in her swollen teats a constant reminder of her loss. Then the milk dried and she mated again, and was consoled by the knowledge of a new litter within her.

That week the weather worsened. A cold wind from the sea swept over the land, bringing rain in its trail. Clouds bulked on the mountains, hiding the peaks, settling on the lower slopes, so that often a chill mist cloaked moor and woodland and hid the loch, and the ground was sodden and the air was moist, and Chia's hunting grounds were boggy and cold. She huddled miserably inside the tree, while water seeped in and the kittens were damp, and sunshine was a distant memory.

Rain swelled the burn. Rain filled the loch. Rain fell on the high slopes, and thin trickles gathered into foaming torrents that raced peatily over the ground, and the hill was alive with noise. The burn was unrecognisable. The tree that spanned it was thrust away from the banks to tumble over the waterfall, and wedge and deepen the pool.

Chia watched the water rise, uneasy and distrustful but reluctant to leave her home. The fifth night of the rains brought a cloud-burst, and she woke from an uneasy half-doze to find an ominous trickle of water at the foot of the tree. The moon shone, briefly bright, silvering the scene, and she stared at the swirl and trembled at the din. She feared nothing that walked, or ran, or flew, but the wildness of weather alarmed her. She could not fight the water or the wind. She could only endure.

The kittens had not yet ventured outside the tree. They were unable to run. They staggered when they walked, tumbling over one another on unsteady legs. When they fell, as they often did, they were astounded and mewed plaintively, annoyed by legs that would not obey their brains. Though so small, the threat of intrusion from the outside world transformed them into scratching, spitting demons. Inside the lair they were balls of fluff, gentle and wide-eyed, with all the charm of domestic kits.

Urgency seized the wildcat. She had to escape from the water, had to take the kittens to safety, and she had to climb. Outside the moon glowed eerily; clouds scudded on the wind and trees moaned, and the roar of the water deadened all other sounds.

The kittens did not understand their mother's sudden extraordinary behaviour. As Chia lifted him, the smallest tom tried to dance away from her, batting at her whiskers with a playful paw. Chia slapped him, knocking him to the ground, and hissed at him. He stared up at her, astounded and, terrified by her anger, dared not move nor murmur when her mouth closed about his scruff and he dangled from her jaws. The wildcat slipped and slithered up the muddy slope, angling away from the water.

She dropped him in a heather-filled hollow, snarling fiercely at him, warning him not to move. She could never risk disobedience, but the kitten's instincts came to her aid. He crouched, cold and lonely, desolately aware of the enormous dark, still as the stones beyond him. He felt unprotected without the warm familiar confines of the tree about him. He shivered. Below her, water crept towards the lair, fingering icily over the ground, reaching for everything that lay in its path. The kittens huddled together, bewildered and afraid, creeping under the heather tumps, hiding from the night.

The last kitten was the greedy female. She had been asleep, having fed full. She woke, and found herself alone. She mewed, craving warmth, desiring the company of her brothers and sisters, needing the reassuring presence of her mother, unnerved by her sudden isolation.

She crept timidly towards the opening that led to the world she had never seen, and stood unsteadily, not yet mistress of her legs. She trembled with fear. The rain had ceased and the clouds parted. Light from the moon poured over the water. The wind rustled and screeched in the trees. The leaves above her head shivered and the inexplicable din of the rapids, thundering over the rocks, appalled her, so that she dared not move.

Chia, some three hundred yards above her, on the hillside, saw the kitten standing in the opening among the roots of the hollow tree. The wildcat mewed and the small head turned towards her.

The owl had her nest in a nearby pine. She was aware of the wildcat and her kittens, but she did not wish to meet the mother. She saw the kitten, unattended, and Chia too far away to intervene. The owl swooped low, feather soft, and was airborne again, her talons loaded. Chia raced towards her and sprang, but missed her mark, She could only watch, fur fluffed, tail bushed, ears flat, as she spat and swore at the creature that had taken her kit. The owl was beyond reach. The kitten was no more than a memory. Chia mourned her, but there was no time for grief.

There was water lapping the tree. Chia raced up the hill. She spent the whole night moving the remaining kits, afraid to leave them out of her sight. The owl had taught her a costly lesson. She carried each kit a few yards, dropped it, and returned for the next, careful never to leave any beyond her reach. There were too many dangers.

She climbed high, away from the water and away from the trees. The kittens did not protest. They were bewildered by their first glimpse of the world and stared without comprehension at the ball of the moon, at the clouding sky, at the vast expanse of the hill and moor, and rock and bush and heather. Twigs and leaves beckoned fascinatingly, shifted by the breeze. Then fascination changed to fear and the immense world threatened, full of unknown terrors. Once, the smallest male, lying in the hollow beside his two sisters, found a beetle. It was satisfying, mysterious, minute, so that he dwarfed it. It moved enticingly. He reached out his paw and tapped at it, entranced by its movements. He was annoyed when Chia, bringing the fourth kitten to join them, mouthed him again in order to carry him higher.

Water lay below them, spread over the flank of the hill. Chia needed sanctuary. Here, where there was little cover, she must have a secure retreat. Danger stalked on four feet; danger flew on strong wings; danger came on two legs, carrying a gun. A hiding place was vital.

She found one at last, an old, deserted fox's den, a deep tunnel sheltered between a tumble of rocks. A stunted bush masked the opening. She carried the first kitten inside, and he bristled, loathing the rank smell that was new to him. Chia hurried away, and brought one of the tiny females to share the nest.

Night was vanishing. Day glinted on the peaks. She was hungry. There had been no time to hunt. She brought the last kitten and curled to rest, letting them suckle, licking each head, aware of her smallest daughter begging for extra affection, tapping at her mother's cheek with an anxious paw. Chia stooped and licked the upturned nose, and sighed deeply. It had been an arduous night, and she was tired. Also she needed food and must hunt by day, or stay hungry for another twelve long hours. She mourned her lost kitten, dozed and dreamed of the owl, and woke to lick anxiously at each small head, caressing them in her own way, aware that there were four, and afraid that while she slept one or more might have vanished and fallen victim in its turn.

The kittens fed, and slept. Chia left them and crept

38

cautiously out of the entrance and on to the hill. She crouched, watching, her tail swinging slowly backwards and forwards along the ground. Far above her the eagle circled, seeing her and noting her. He knew that where the cat laired, there would be bounty. He was hunting for his own young, newly hatched, and for his mate. He needed food.

Chia crouched in the heather. Nothing moved but her eyes. There were deer feeding on the slopes; seven hinds, six of them in calf. One stood, sentinel, looking about her, ears fanning for sound, nose questioning the wind. The wind brought the scent of seawrack and of thyme, bruised by the herd; the dank sour-sweet smell of the drowning ground on the lower slopes, and the scent of another small group of hinds beyond a rise and out of sight. It brought no news of the wildcat to the grazing beasts. She had been too careful. She had the wind in her face, telling her of the hinds, of a stag, lying up in deep heather on his own, and of a hare, crouched within yards of where Chia lay.

She began to stalk. Legs bent, almost flat on the ground, moving ghostlike, step by slow step, heart beating wildly as excitement built inside her, saliva forming in her mouth, hunger an overpowering frenzy, she schooled herself. She needed every mite of experience, every care, and perfect judgement.

The hare was suckling a leveret. She too had read the wind and knew of the deer. She did not know of the wildcat. She did not scent her, nor hear her, nor see her until Chia sprang. The hare struggled violently, hind legs kicking and thrusting. She tried to bite. The leveret was crushed beneath his mother. The deer fled. Soon the hare's lifeless body was stretched beside her son and the wildcat fed greedily, tearing at the warm flesh, soothing her hunger. She finished eating in the shelter of a gorse bush and left the carcase, and returned to the mouth of the den, where she luxuriated in the sun that had risen over the peaks and warmed the morning. She cleaned herself meticulously and purred softly, but she did not relax her watch.

She saw the eagle stoop from the sky and rescue the remains of her meal. He was another enemy, possibly more dangerous than the man. She had not met eagles before. She basked, languorous, filled and content. The eagle had gone. Nothing moved before her or above her. The day was hers.

Her smallest daughter came to look for her. Chia watched the tiny creature stand, dazzled, in the sunlight, narrowing her eyes. The wind blew, ruffling her coat, and she spat, a minute body powered by ferocity. Chia reached a lazy paw and patted the kit, and greeted her, nose against nose. The kitten burrowed into her mother's coat and hid from the intense light. The world was too much for her. She needed comfort.

Chia mewed. One by one, the other kittens came to her, sharply aware of the wind on their fur, the unseen stroking fingers baffling them, so that each in turn, copied the first, and spat. Chia bathed them with her tongue and they curled against her, savouring the sunshine, worshipping the warmth, yet at the least sound, transformed, so that ears flattened against their heads, eyes glared and each tiny mouth opened in a vicious snarl.

Each was different. The biggest male, Silver, had a gleam of grey in his fluffy coat, that did not as yet reveal his future adult markings. His brother, Fury, intensely fierce, ready to fight the sun, the moon, and the dancing maddening shadows of grasses that moved in the wind, spent his days spitting in minuscule wrath.

The little female, Jade, clinging close, needing her mother more than the others, was wary of everything that walked in the wild, and cried forlornly whenever she was left alone, begging Chia to return, to hurry back to her, to tell her that all was well. Her green eyes were a clear beautiful colour, resembling the gemstone. Her sister, Amber, had eyes tinged with yellow.

Chia's world centred on the den beneath the rocks. She came out each evening, when bats flittered among the trees, and the tiny pipistrelles hawked for insects. The kittens watched the bats, enthralled, fascinated by their swift movements, sometimes pouncing and striking, unaware that the distance between them and the flittering beasts that quartered the air was too great for capture.

Fury explored the area immediately around the den. He was far more curious than the others, vigorously alive and intensely mischievous. He stopped at every sound, to crouch, to snarl, to spit, so that his forays were exhausting, his small heart racing constantly as fear mastered him. Only slowly did he learn that the mysterious unseen wind that played in his fur, annoying him, and bringing strange scents, was harmless in itself. Once, when the breeze advertised a questing fox, heavy-pawed as he ran along the hard-packed trail, Chia hissed at the kits and drove them into the den and crouched over them, her ears flat, her throat throbbing with a half-uttered snarl. The fox was Old Scarface. He heard her, paused to identify the sound, and loped on hastily, not wishing to challenge her. It was some time before she relaxed and allowed the kittens to venture into the moonlight.

Fury now knew the smell of fox. He stored it in his memory. Silver knew it too, but he was less wary than his brother and often, when he was playing with a leaf or a broken twig, Chia had to slap him in order to drive him home. He was heedless, and she needed to guard him, chide him, and watch him constantly.

Jade never moved far from her mother and always obeyed at once, running when she was called, eager to lift her face and nuzzle Chia's lips and nose, curling close at night, manoeuvring so that it was always she who lay between the wildcat's forepaws, close against her chest, tucked beneath her chin. It was always Amber who was last to come, who dallied to watch a branch dip in the air, or to investigate, with curved paw, some insect that had crawled into a cranny in the rocks. It was always Fury who woke first and hissed and spat, alerting the rest of the family, as he heard a cry in the dark, or the thudding hooves of a running deer, or a pulse-racing call of a hunting owl, flighting down the hill. Often Fury woke again and spat at the cry of mouse or baby rabbit, as the owl caught his prey, and the night was briefly horrid with death.

Later that month the wildcat cherished the four kits in her lair. It was a dangerous night, a cold night in mid-May, the full moon revealing the world, every movement clear for watching eyes to see. Chia hunted briefly, and killed a rabbit and brought it home to feed. The kittens were not yet ready for meat but they licked at the blood and chewed the paws. Fury had a rabbit tail of his own, that he used as a toy and teased and carried, and tucked beneath him when he went to sleep. None of the others was allowed to touch it. He snarled at them and bit Silver when he tried to steal the trophy.

Chia dozed, fed and comfortable. There was nothing moving outside. She re-lived her kill, which had been a young beast, unwary, bounding in moon madness over the dewy grass, ignoring the thump of alarm from the old buck as he smelled cat and fled for his burrow.

The kittens tugged at her. She stirred and purred briefly and dozed again, and woke to clean each small beast thoroughly. They were soon damp from the ministrations of her busy tongue. When she had finished all four slept and Chia relaxed, and dreamed again, but startled to attention when she heard Fury spit and snarl. The snarl was low, throaty, and continuous, as terror dominated him, yet it was still a baby sound which would not strike fear into any hunter's heart. Chia crouched, listening, and her own pulses pounded. Ears flattened, lips drawn back, eyes narrowed, she shielded her kits, and they woke and listened to the noises on the hill, and Jade crept close for company, pressing herself against her mother's leg.

The galloping hooves fled past the sanctuary; they heard the sounds of agony from a tortured throat, the terror panting of the creature in the night and the pad, pad, pad, and heavy breathing of the beast that followed. Fury had never heard anything like it. His senses told him that there was panic out there in the dark; he caught the echoes and felt his mother's thumping heart, and her soft snarl confirmed that there was danger. Danger such as he had never seen or dreamed of in his brief life. He stored the knowledge.

The wind brought the scent of the running beasts to them. Chia identified deer and fox, and relaxed, knowing that she was not threatened. Fury was not reassured. He crouched beside her, wild with fear, and listened to the scream of the tortured deer, and the dull thump of its body as it fell, shaking the ground. It was an injured beast, the imprint of death already upon it, and the fox found an easy kill.

The wildcat had fed well the night before. She did not need to hunt again. She stayed in the den. When Chia slept

42

Fury left her, for though he was frightened, he was also curious and brave. He was growing, was alert and restless and he longed to see more of the noisy mysterious world. He crept to the mouth of the den. The moon rode up the sky, full-fledged and fascinating. He stared at it, watching the wind tease clouds to shreds and mottle the golden face. He listened, ears pricked forward. There was fear abroad in the dark, fear so tangible and horrid that he knew its chill touch, and backed away from the entrance.

Chia heard the rumour of wings, and Fury's sudden desperate mew. She bounded to the opening, grabbed the kit by the loose fur of his scruff, and pulled him inside, and the owl, flying mute and snowflake-silent on the moonglim, missed his mark and landed heavily against the rock, bruising himself, and was angered. He flew off, calling, owl moan answering owl moan, as his mate hunted on the far side of the burn, looking for fieldmice and short-tailed voles. Fury lay beside his mother, trembling. He had no urge to venture further that night.

During the next few days, the kittens began to explore. Chia watched them anxiously, remembering how her third daughter had died, knowing that all her first litter had vanished. Danger was everywhere; from owl and eagle; from fox and from man. She had not seen the keeper for some days, but she had not forgotten him nor the gun that he carried.

She took the kittens out to play at dusk and dawn. They fought and wrestled and bit; they found twigs and leaves and dry grass stems and chased after them. They learned to stalk Chia's tail and catch it, and when she came back from hunting they raced to meet her, falling over one another in eagerness to greet her, but Jade was always first.

They learned to know the approaches to the den; the way up the slippery rocks on the western side, facing the setting sun. The dark-streaked flying clouds of night enthralled them, and they sat staring, wide-eyed, and then turned, concentration ended, to watch a leaf at the end of a twig move mysteriously against the trunk of the old tree that the wind had twisted into a snarl of branches, and that had rooted under the rocks that hid the entrance to the den, and to flash at it with excited, inexpert paws.

They learned the path to the water, and they learned to lap. The way was devious, leading from the den through a maze of close-growing whinberry bushes, under an arching bramble, through thick rank grass, and at last to the slide of shingle where the bank of the burn had worn away, leaving a level patch that led to shallows, tumbling breathlessly over worn rock, safe for a kit to explore and not deep enough to tempt any other questing creature. It was a long trail for the kittens, and fraught with terror, as unidentifiable noises constantly threatened their safety.

The wildcat guarded them as they drank at dawn, and if the sky were marred by hovering eagle, or kestrel or merlin hung above, her swift hiss and snarl sent them scurrying into the shelter of the bushes, where they crouched, wide-eyed, in deceptive placidity that was soon betrayed as some beast came too near, and each kitten transformed itself into a spitting replica of Chia, who stood above them, enlarged by anger, ready to pounce, to fight, and to kill.

CHAPTER FOUR

The golden eagle hung on the air. His eyes watched the ground for movement; slide of weasel, slither of stoat, or stumble of cub or kitten. His mate was guarding the downling, newly hatched, its head too heavy for its body. It lay flat among the tangle of twigs that had grown on the rocky ledge at the peak of the hill. The mother bird brought green branches, in new spring leaf, and thrust them among the vast raft which sheltered the fledgling.

The youngster was female. She had been hatched for over a week and her pleading cries brought the male frequently to the nest with offerings of rabbit and mouse, which his mate shredded, and held out to the little creature. It was covered in soft down, and it watched eagerly for food.

The father hunted constantly. His keen eyes noted the slip of green grass stems that betrayed a creature moving below. His swift plunge took the prowler by surprise, and death was no more than a cessation of life, coming clean and quick in the guise of a thunderbolt leased from the sky. There was no pause for pain. There was no time for realisation.

When food was plentiful and hunting easy, the male relaxed in play. He soared and swooped joyously, riding the air streams, saving his energy. Wings folded, he dived through the brilliant air, until it seemed he would hit the ground and end his life. The wings opened, the fall was braked and he soared again, and stood sentinel above the nest, watchful. He had little to fear.

The cheep of his hungry youngster drove him to the air again, and his shadow brought quaking fear to those groundlings that saw it. The wary hid. The unwary died.

Beyond the eagle's eyrie was a sparrowhawk's nest. The hawk also had young to feed. He brought smaller prey and, one early morning, he and his mate unintentionally brought food to Chia.

The male bird saw a pigeon wing across the top of the wood. The female was tired of the nest and wanted to change from brooding her young. She left them briefly and followed her mate. She saw him head the smaller bird towards her and dived at it. The pigeon changed direction, its heart thumping. It was a homer, blown off course while racing home to its owner.

The hawks chivvied it between them, now soaring, now diving, now heading it one way, now another, until the bird, frantic, flew into the shelter of the trees, plunging downwards, and ran along the ground trying to dodge its pursuers.

Chia was lying in a sunny patch outside the mouth of her lair. The kittens were asleep and she was resting. Her quick ears heard the patter of the bird and the thump of its heart. She moved lazily, sinuously, blending with the trunk of the tree beside her, a pattern of light and shade that seemed part of the surroundings, a movement of dappled body that was no more obtrusive than the shake of leaves in the shadows on the grass. The pigeon was concentrating on the hawks. The male dived low and Chia sprang. The baffled hawk screeched his rage, braked sharply, and soared upwards, frustrated, as Chia took the pigeon and ate it in the dark entrance to her lair. The feathers blew in the wind and the kittens played with the quills.

By now the world, for the kits, was wild excitement. They emerged at dusk, and learned to identify sounds. Sound was the most important part of their world, and their hearing guarded them from dangers that sight might overlook. They did not see as well as the birds; for them, movement was paramount, and creatures that lay still were safe from their depredations. Movement was betrayal; the twist of a tail, the flirt of a grass stem, the slink of small furry beast, or the rush and run of a beetle along the secret trails between the grasses was enough to alert each wildkit, so that their unsteady legs led them to mimic pounce and inexpert unrewarded attempts to kill.

Noise! Chia, listening, identified running fox and bounding deer; flight of heron and flit of bat; soar of eagle and swoop of hawk; the unalarming slur of leaves against a tree trunk, or the thrash of bracken as an irritable stag pawed the earth with his hoof. She knew the sound of the hinds as they browsed, the rustle and squeak that betrayed mice in the grasses, the bark of a fox in the night, the bleat of a new-born lamb calling to its mother. She knew the chitter and twitter of birdsong, betraying the singer, the flutter of wings as the bird flew to its nest, the cheep of chicks in the grass, brooded by the mother grouse, the sharp sawing alarm calls of the frantic birds when they saw her, the cawing screech of the heron as he winged to his nest.

She taught the kits to distinguish windnoise and treenoise from owlnoise and hawknoise; to listen for the heart-quickening squeak that betrayed prey in the bushes; to know the feel of fur against their teeth, as she brought them small creatures to worry.

She dragged her tail along the ground, willing them to jump at it, and strengthen their legs and learn to use eye and pouncing paw together, so that each leap was practice for the life that must be theirs when they grew and she no longer watched over them and hunted for them.

She rolled on the ground, teasing at them, so that they leaped at her and battled with her in mimic fury, and the kittens growled while Chia purred, indulgent, knowing that this was training and brought them skill.

The mock fights always ended with grooming, and Chia washed each until satisfied with her work; cleaning eyes and nose and ears, until the kits protested and struggled to free themselves and she let them go and attended to the next.

There was so much to hear, to smell, to see. Early one morning, venturing further than usual from the lair, one of the kits paused with paw uplifted and looked back at Chia. She was at his side on the instant, scarcely seeming to move, her ears already aware of the rustle on the ground.

There was a young weasel in the clearing. He was more than half-grown and merry with vitality, spinning in a whirl of paw and tail, chasing his own tail, apparently oblivious to everything around him.

On bush and branch the birds sat, watching, fascinated

by the wheeling body that twisted and turned in a mazy dance, that enticed the kittens as well as the birds. They crept forward, intrigued.

Chia hissed.

There was a clamour of bird note and the kits rushed to stand beside their mother. The weasel stared at the wildcat, furious, head up, mouth open, and then, eel-like, he vanished into the undergrowth, leaving only a memory and the knowledge that here was danger, the certainty of fear, which the kits caught from their mother, whose bristling fur and snarling mouth showed them her own reaction as plainly as if she had spoken to them. They ran to hide. Hiding was sanctuary, was darkness, was release from danger. Hiding was warm milk and soft furry bodies, and their mother's reassuring throaty purr. Hiding was sleep, and the security of the walls of earth that sheltered them, and the dry rustle of the dead leaves and soft moss and fur with which Chia lined their bed.

It was dark before the wildcat allowed the kits to move again. Outside in the misty night the moon was a remote glitter on veiling clouds. The wind was a whisper on the gently sliding leaves; there were soft rustles and swift furtive movements on the ground; there was the call of the sea, surging on the distant beach, and the fine edge of a rainstorm that lowered over the peak, but here was no more than a rumour, barely wetting the kits' soft fluffy coats.

Chia crouched beside the kittens, listening and watching. Soon she would drive them back, warning them to stay in the den, while she hunted, but now she let them play, and guarded them from danger.

Danger was stalking over the hill. The polecat was hunting too. She crept downwards, in a drift of scent that was dispelled by the wind that told only those behind her of her passing. Her paws moved silently over the ground, but not so silently that Chia did not hear her as she came near. The wildcat did not wait. A spit and a hiss, and a paw slapped at a tardy kitten, and no sign of the family was left in the clearing. The kits were safe in their lair and Chia guarded the entrance, enraged and ready to kill. The polecat did not see her. She ran down the hill, to forage over the moor, hunting the rabbits that were scarce and becoming scarcer.

The wind blew the last trace of cloud from the sky. The moon cast deep shadows and the kits crept out to watch the night. Chia played with them, and then drove them inside again, and hunted swiftly, her paws eager. She killed several mice and found a nest filled with eggs, deserted by the mother. She broke the eggs and licked the contents avidly. She watched the owl fly over the moor, aware of the swish of his wings in the air. He flew away from her and she relaxed. He threatened her peace of mind, as he could easily take another of the kittens to his brood. As yet, they were very small and totally vulnerable.

They were temptation to the vixen, hunting for her cubs; to the questing owl and the stoat and the weasel; to the soaring eagle and the hovering hawk; they were threatened by the viper, sliding softly through the grass; they were food for the hoodie crow, that would peck out their eyes, as he pecked the eyes of newborn weakly lambs. There was no safety in the world until they were grown, and even then there was man and his gun and his dogs.

Chia hurried back, and nosed among the kits, counting them, making sure each one was safe, was there, was waiting for her. They would soon be bold and venture alone, and they had so little knowledge. She tucked herself in among them and cherished them and purred.

Outside the lair the moon vanished and day gilded the sky and the eagle soared, watching, and plunged and found a newborn deer, dropped early. He swept up again, his talons empty, as the hind raced at him, berserk. She stood on her hindlegs, driving at him with her forelegs, and he abandoned the quest, leaving her to run to the calf and nose it, and reassure herself that all was well, and bark a warning so that other hinds were alerted and the bird soared, hungry, and his youngster screamed for food and was not fed. His eyes watched intently and twice the wind betrayed him. It was strong enough to move the bushes and the bird thought that the shifting leaves revealed a hidden source of food and dived, only to find that he had been mistaken. Rain, driving suddenly from the west, wetted him and he sulked above his nest, knowing that every creature would seek shelter and that hunting was futile. The female brought new leafy branches to mesh into the pattern of the nest. She liked to add them daily as they died. She tore at the leaves, frustrated, while the youngster cheeped unavailingly.

Not till mid-afternoon did the rain clear and the sun glance briefly from a marbled sky, and the hidden creatures begin to move on the ground. The eagle plunged at the shaking grass, and was rewarded. He brought a weasel kit to his mate and she tore it for the clamouring fledgling that was already learning to tear food for itself. The eaglet had grown to an ugly creature, that now stood on the nest and mantled its food with its wings, hiding it from its parents, threatening them with its beak if they came near, afraid that they would snatch the food from it. Its brother had hatched a few days before, been ruthlessly attacked, and had died. The parents took no heed. There was seldom enough food for more than one fledgling, and only once in the twelve years that they had been mates had they raised two. Then rabbits had been so thick on the hill that there was food in plenty and every hunter flourished.

CHAPTER FIVE

Chia watched her kittens grow; she noted each achievement; she guarded them as they played, stretching herself on a lichened rock where she could see everything that moved on either side and before her. She made certain that the wind was her watchdog and brought swift news of beasts behind her. The family was not yet old enough to take hunting.

Pride mastered her, and she purred softly to herself as the kits fought and bit, grappling together in feigned anger, sometimes in a tumble of paws and tails, at others two by two. Silver always struggled to overcome his smaller and more agile brother; Jade chased Amber, engaging her in trials of strength that lasted only seconds and ended with the two females pressed together, lying side by side, purring contentedly.

When play was over Chia leaped down beside them and led them into the den, dug deep beneath the tumbled rocks. Here all five curled close and slept through the bright hours of day. Chia herself lay in a half-doze, aware of the albino stag, who avoided the herd and lived in loneliness among the bilberry bushes and the heather, and often grazed near the rocks; aware of the stoat slipping downhill on some urgent quest of his own; aware of the rustle of the wind in the shrubby undergrowth that masked the entrance to her lair.

She listened, always, for the thud of the man's boots on the ground, and the jingle of the tab on Bran's collar, inaudible to Fergus, but, to the wildcat, presenting a faint but insistent warning. Any unrecognised movement raced her heart and startled her to instant vigilance, which was only relaxed when the sounds were identified. She listened for the urgent yak yak from the birds that haunted the mountain. The threat might be from hunting hawk or prowling fox, or the eagle waiting to fill the maw of his growing youngster that screamed and opened its wide-gaped mouth for food and yet more food. The great bird knew where the wildkits hid. He wheeled in the air, a feathered presage of doom, and below him the creatures that laired on the hill trembled and crept out of sight, each one terrified of the winged death that swept pitilessly out of the sky.

Whenever the kits were playing and the eagle loured, Chia hissed them to safety. They learned to look up, and to fear him, although they did not yet know why. They had never witnessed his arrogant stoop. Always Amber was the last kit home, mesmerised by movement; by the shadows that fled over the ground as the wind tore the cloud shreds; by the entrancing dip and sway of a grass blade, asking to be tapped and caught and eaten; by the dancing wind-blown feathers that she could not resist chasing. Chia hissed, and slapped with an outraged paw, and caught her daughter by the scruff and carried her inside against her will, but still Amber tarried.

When the kits were six weeks old Chia left them, as usual, to go hunting. They taxed all her strength now that they were growing, and she was ravenous. The youngsters were already teasing at the mice and young rabbits that she brought, and she needed larger prey to fill her.

She saw the hare prancing in May-moon madness in the clearing beyond the burn. Twisting and turning, leaping sideways and bounding high, he performed by himself, unaware of passing time that lightened the sky with dawn, or eyes that watched him from the bushes. He was young and not yet wise.

Belly low, crouching, Chia crept towards him, scarcely shivering the grasses. She had crawled beyond the wind and his scent was in her nose. Her scent was blown behind her, and the hare knew nothing of her presence. His final leap brought him to within five feet of her and she sprang. He died in a kick of legs and a sudden panic that was stifled before he had time to recognise the fate that had overtaken him. Chia dragged his body up the hill.

Dawn reddened the sky and sun trails shone in the burn.

The kittens, waiting, were playing in the light of day, heedless and unaware. Silver and Fury chased each other's tails and sparred until they were breathless. Fury, suddenly angered beyond bearing, bit his brother's ear, drawing blood. Silver yowled and slashed at the smaller kit's nose. Seconds later the fight was forgotten and each was licking the other's wound.

Jade was watching for the wildcat. Always anxious, she had poised herself on the hillside, half hidden under a rock, so that she would be the first to see her mother return. She was aware of scent from the heather, and from bruised thyme trodden by a hind that had passed that way before the light betrayed her presence. There was a drift of sea-wrack on the air. Then, doom-laden, fright-provoking, death-threatening, came the throat-tightening tang and terrifying slither of weasel. Jade hissed. Her brothers heard her, obeyed the warning, and ran to the den, where the three sheltered, ears flat, mouths snarling, small hearts thumping in painful fear.

Amber was playing with a trail of straw that had been blown for miles by the wind. It teased her and mocked her, mousetail straw, rattail straw. It was prey, it was victim, and her tapping paw would bring it death. She pounced as the wind snatched it from her, and grabbed, holding it down with both front paws. She took it in her teeth and, bewilderingly, there were two mousetails both twisting away from her, distracting her, so that she did not know which one to stalk.

She was overwhelmed by the sudden appalling weasel-scent as she darted after the nearest straw-tail. She leaped, twisting swiftly, electrified, as she saw the slender body, the bright wicked eyes, and the eager many-toothed mouth that gaped at her in a grin of desire. The lolling tongue was wet. She dropped the straw and fluffed her fur until she was three times normal size, a-snarl with fury that was fed by terror, one clawed paw lifted ready to slash. The banshee squeal of enraged small cat fed the greedy air, and was blown on the whirling wind. Chia heard. She dropped the hare and raced up the hill on paws quickened by fear.

The weasel hesitated. Amber was armed, able to fight and bite although she was so small. The eagle saw them and his own heart thundered his excitement. He speeded his wing-beats and streamed down the sky, the air roaring behind him. Chia streaked towards her kit. Her screech of rage alerted the weasel. He turned his head. Amber fled for the rocks and Chia pounced, but missed the eel-like body that twisted away from her. The eagle was upon them, not having seen her come. The weasel hung from his talons as the huge bird struggled to rise. The unexpected trophy was larger than the wildkit and meant more food for the half-fledged creature that dominated the nest and shrieked when it saw its father riding the slipstream.

Chia drove Amber into the den, and returned to look for the dead hare. It had vanished, found by the vixen, running home, late and starving, to her own cubs. She had taken it, greedy for such unexpected largesse. Chia quartered the ground in vain, puzzled by its absence, then caught the foxscent and knew the search futile. That day the wildcat went hungry, hunting while the sky was light, feeding on tiny mice and a small bird that fluttered unwarily on a bush nearby. She leaped and knocked it out of the air as it flew. It was a meagre mouthful.

The kittens had learned a lesson. Amber, when night brought moonlight to flood the hill, had not yet recovered from fright. The weasel's teeth had been too near; the eagle, rushing through the air, had set her blood pumping fast, and even now, hours later, the fur of her tail was fluffed and when the other kits moved she hissed at them. She would never forget.

When her brothers and sister went out to play she crouched among the rocks, and every sound, and every hoofbeat, sent her further into the safety of darkness, into the quiet familiar lair where she listened and watched and sorted the scents on the wind, now warier even than Fury.

Twice Fury's warning sent the kits to shelter. Once a long-legged fox raced by, intent on his own business; once a running deer, far away but plainly heard, roused their fears. They hid and waited for Chia to come.

Chia was no longer merely hungry. She was ravenous. Her empty belly ached. Food was a driving urgency, a raging need, and to suffer longer was a penance she could not endure. Hares and rabbits were scarce on the ground and the hinds guarded the calves too well. There were now several new-born on the hill. There were roebuck kids, but the roe were clever and although she stalked one, a buck kicked her and her ribs were afire with bruises. A scant mile away Fergus kept his ducks and hens and geese. There were pheasant chicks in the pens and red grouse in the bushes.

She ran through tussocky heather and avoided the brambles that snatched at her fur. She found a dozy mouse and paused, and killed, and ate, but it was a pitiful thing, a mouthful that barely assuaged the pangs that ripped her. Saliva drooled on her lips and she licked them hastily.

She scented Dragon, hunting on his own, revelling in the night. She waited, silent. If she went down the hill now he might attack her. The noise would betray her presence. Dragon had found a young rabbit that had never learned fear. The old cat washed the blood trace from his jaws with a careful paw and loped away. Chia finished the kill, but Dragon had left little. She stalked on, purposeful.

The stone house was silent, but the warm glow of an oil lamp spilled gold from the windows beside the front door. Tim, always conscious of telltale taint or movement, pricked his ears, uneasy, as the wind, unusually warm, drifted in through the window, redolent with scent. He gave a small half-bark to alert Fergus and Bran caught his excitement, and full of misguided enthusiasm chased to the window and barked joyously, glad of an opportunity to give tongue. Fergus quieted the dog. The Jack Russell listened, head cocked, ears pricked, intent. Rob sat, his eyes watchful.

The man stood by the open window. He heard nothing but the sough in the trees and, far away, the soft swell and suck of the waves on the beach of the loch. An owl whooped downwind. The wildcat was crouched in thick bushes, her eyes wide, watching the house. Chia was as silent as the shadows that sped across the ground, thrown by clouds that played beneath the moon, clouds that were building into rainstorm, and tattered by the wind that flung their streamers across the midnight sky.

There was a faint rustle, and Dragon came from the little garden behind the house, looked expectantly up at Fergus, and jumped in through the window.

'It's only Dragon, you soft beasts,' the keeper said, and whistled the dogs upstairs. The dogs followed him, puzzled, knowing that the wildcat lurked in the darkness. They could not make the keeper understand and twice he quieted them, irritated.

The wildcat saw the glow die in the downstairs window. She heard the man's heavy footsteps and the following paws padding on the uncarpeted stone steps. She saw the brief glim that shone in the bedroom and was swiftly dowsed. Her fur was ruffled as the wind filled her nose with the taste of duck and chicken and pheasant and grouse and she could not control the slaver in her mouth. She licked her lips avidly, striving to master excitement that was mounting to a peak.

When darkness reassured her she glided through the shadows, using every scrap of cover. A thin rain began to fall, wetting her coat. She was aware of owlcall in the distance. She found a trace of Dragon on the ground and veered away from it, not wishing to meet him. The pens were at the back of the house. She leaped the garden wall and the smell of the fowl reeked all round her, the air thick and pungent, and saliva dripped from her mouth. She circled the pens. The wire was strong and firmly anchored. There was no way in.

She tried biting, tugging at the unrelenting caging, but the metal defied her teeth. She clawed, but although it moved to her muscular paw it did not give way. Fergus had reinforced all the fencing, until it was as safe as armour plating, and to make doubly sure he had bought a gander from the farm. The old bird heard her. He lifted his head. A moment later the wind betrayed the sound of her and told him that Chia was there, and the din he made startled the other birds to idiot clamour, set Bran and Tim barking, drove Jackie to the window to add his sharper note, and brought Fergus from his bed, half blind with sleep and yawning.

The wildcat did not wait. She knew the man would come and bring his gun. Long before the door was open she was away on the moors, her hunger greater than ever. She ran, bounding lightly, pausing at intervals to smell the wind and to listen. Rain lashed from the sky. Rain washed away the scent on the ground. Rain sent small beasts to shelter, mice into crannies and cracks and holes, rabbits to their burrows, hares to crouch in their forms, watching, ears fanned to detect the smallest sound. They would hear creak and rustle and whisper, no matter how faint.

At the edge of the moor was a young plantation. The conifers, no higher than a red stag's head, grew in formed and serried lines. A well-kept fence kept the deer from spoiling the young shoots. Chia circled the barrier, and then threw up her head. There was a deer, crying, near by. The sorrowing bleats called her on. She ran lightly.

A still-born calf lay on the ground. The hind mourned, unable to believe her loss or to reconcile herself to the fact that her baby was dead. Chia watched, but the wind betrayed her and, maddened by fear and grief, the bereaved hind raced towards her, standing on her hindlegs, intending to smash her forelegs on to the wildcat's back. Chia recognised her intention and fled. The deer returned to her calf and wailed to the heartless sky.

Chia hunted until daybreak, without success. The little creatures were wary. At dawn the hungry wildcat slipped quietly through the trees and crossed the moor. The kits were waiting for her. Jade ran to greet her, to fuss her, to welcome her with uplifted nose and frantic purr and a paw that patted at Chia's face, as if the little beast had to make certain her mother was there, was real, had returned and was not the uncertain image of a dream. Amber waited in the shelter of the rocks. The eagle hung in the sky; though he was distant and intent on other prey, she had not forgotten her fright and at times her sleep was marred by the memory of his wings plunging towards her in a roar of sound, and she woke fear-filled and crept closer to her mother, and lay watchful, alert, listening to the daytime sounds that penetrated the lair.

Fury and Silver greeted Chia, fought amicably, and followed her inside. Day threatened their safety. Day showed them to the other creatures that hunted on the hills. Day was a traitor never to be trusted, though at times, when the sun was hot, the cat took the kits and they curled in a densely shrubby hollow, where the heat warmed a patch of soft earth and where, if murder came stalking, she could instantly hide in safety, running as soon as her senses warned her of an enemy. The kits had now experienced danger and her quick hiss sent them into sanctuary, where they crouched, motionless, ready to spit defiance, to snarl in rage, to claw in desperate battle. Time passed, aiding her, ensuring that they were stronger, and already their claws were capable of inflicting severe damage.

That night Chia went to the moor, avoiding the man-place. She caught a large rat and four mice. She ate the rat but brought the mice home, one by one, without killing them. She freed them in front of the kittens, and watched as each played with a living trophy. They had never had live prey near them before. They were in a little clearing immediately below the entrance to the den.

Fury stretched his paw and tapped his mouse on the muzzle. It squealed in panic. Fury's eyes were bright, his head inquisitive. He sniffed the mouse, which ran, terrified, away from the reek of cat. The kitten tapped the warm body again. The game palled. He did not associate the living creature with food and let it run. Chia caught it, and brought it back to him and killed it in front of him. Then he recognised the taste and smell of warm blood, and began to lick at the dead body.

The other kittens were alerted by the tang and left their prey, and tried to take his from him. He was instant rage, snarling at them, justifying his name, so that they left him in peace. Chia killed the remaining mice and each kit took one, but Jade left hers and shared companionably with Amber. Chia ate the last, crouched over it, on the lookout rock. Not even while she was feeding did she relax, and as the old Scarface ran down the trail, his telltale aura betraying him, she hissed and the family fled to shelter, each kitten carrying a trophy. Fury had finished eating his mouse and retrieved his rabbit tail, filthy with age and licking, but still well-cherished. Jade carried a feather, leaving the mouse remains to Amber.

Deep beneath the rocks they slept, and Chia guarded them. Each hour of safety was a small triumph; each day gave her a stake for the future; each week brought new strength to her young. This time her kittens might survive. Her own store of wisdom was greater. She had experienced much since her first litter died and, although she was incapable of formulating thought, she had knowledge; she could learn and remember, and teach the kitten to avoid the pitfalls that trapped the unwary.

CHAPTER SIX

The kittens' sixth week was memorable. Fergus, quartering the hills in his work, hoping also to find the wildcat and her young, was increasingly aware of the weather. Rain came daily from sodden skies. He was wet and weary, and his clothes were never dry. Once he found the wildcat's pawmark near the new plantation, but the ground was saturated and did not carry scent, and the dogs lost her track on rock. Chia was clever and knew how to confuse her trail. She often took to the trees.

The dogs smelled her several times but they could not tell the man that the reek was wildcat and not fox. He thought that they warned him of Old Scarface, who had signed his own death warrant by killing two lambs. Both were sickly and dying, but spilled blood told the keeper that the fox had anticipated and killed living creatures. He left his pad marks, plain to see, in the mud beside the kills. This time the wildcat was not to blame. All the same, if she found newly dead lambs she might change her diet. An hour-old lamb would be easy prey.

Chia was aware of the man, and even more aware of his gun. She watched him from high in a tree, sprawled along a thick branch, intrigued by the bird that flew in front of Fergus and then flew back to alight on his shoulder. Tip enjoyed accompanying his master but his excursions were rare. He was much too quick to call his warning, not to the prowling beast that had alerted him, but to the keeper who was now Tip's family and needed protection in just the same way.

All week the wind screamed on the hill. It pounded the loch and mountainous waves, backed by the increasing gale, brought each tide higher, so that soon there were flooded roads and strangers had to make detours that took them up the forestry track through Chia's territory. She eyed the cars with dislike, and ran from the searching headlights that raked towards her as she hunted. She knew Fergus's Land-Rover, but had never seen any other vehicle.

On the third night of the gale, when wind lashed the trees, a car, bound for a distant town, hit an unwary hare that was racing across the road. Chia had become used to the cars and was curious. Watching from the edge of the bushes, she saw it die, and recognised that the strange and noisy object that shed brilliance from its great eyes was yet another killer, as deadly as the gun.

She waited until the engine note had faded on the air and, as the road was now deserted, took the hare to her den. The meat was unexpected and very welcome. She watched the kits tear and harry and bite, and fight one another for the food. She listened uneasily as she watched. She had never heard such wind.

All night the gale raged. A giant pine, which had long been a landmark on the hill, crashed to the ground. The earth shook. The kittens forgot the hare and crept to Chia for comfort. She was also afraid and drove them down, into the earth, away from the dreadful noise.

The trees rustled and raged, and bent to the ground, flung turbulent heads and creaked protesting branches. Terrified birds clinging, shaken, to their uneasy shelter, added their voices to the din, so that all were awake and their plaints echoed eerily above the howl of the gale. Owl cried and heron cried and the wood pigeons cowered and crooned. Alarm notes and fear notes chattered incessantly, sounding throughout the storm.

A bough, torn from a rowan tree, crashed downwards, and the squirrel crashed with it, her new-born young dying as they hit the rocky soil. She leaped clear and crouched in the shelter of a bush that swayed about her, and mourned bitterly, grief added to terror, and trunks bent and grasses were flattened and twigs were hurled from the sky.

Thunder rolled. Lightning flared. The underground den where the kittens lay trembling, close against Chia, was briefly brilliant with blinding light. The wildcat had heard thunder before but never known a night like this. Her heart raced and she licked each kit in turn, deriving comfort from their presence. The falling pine had shaken the ground. Small trickles of earth fell into the den, one of them increasing to a minor landslide.

Desperately afraid, Chia forced the kits outside. Weather was a constant threat to every creature that laired on the hill. Lightning blinded the five of them. Chia did not know where to turn or where to run for safety. She crouched with the kits under the lee of a rock, watching. She had been wise to leave. The earthfalls increased and the ground caved in. The paths at the entrance slid deep inside. Had she remained she and her family would have been crushed together, and their history ended.

On the slope above the crouching wildcats was an isolated tree. It had long forgotten the sap of spring and leafless, dead, pointed sere branches at the clouds. Lightning scythed from the sky and it split with a crack that terrified every beast within hearing; its falling trunk dislodged a rock that pounded down the hill.

This was a new terror and, even worse, it could not be identified. The kittens were enlarged with fear, every hair erect, ears flat, eyes narrowed. The sound pursued them, rumbling slowly at first and then, as the hill steepened, the boulder gathered impetus and thundered towards them, rolling unevenly, twisting away from its original path, deflected by other rocks, which were collected in its progress until a tumble of granite was pouring down the slope.

There was nothing to do but run. Chia hissed at the kittens to follow her. They sped through the darkness. They were not yet fleet, and she had to stop and ensure that they were behind her, not once but many times.

The wind rocked the bushes that grew around them. The rain soaked their fur. The ground was boggy and running was not easy; paws slipped into water that the kittens hated. But terror did not wait. It stalked beside them, driving them on, as the roar of the growing avalanche mounted deafeningly, and none of them could hear their mother's voice.

Fury led them, following as fast as he knew. He was sodden within minutes, small half-drowned kit, bony and pathetic, soaked fur flat about him. He wanted warmth and comfort and all he knew was the wicked gale that screamed and raged through the trees, that flattened his fur and checked his progress. He shivered as he stumbled along. He was often forced to crouch flat, as the wind hurled itself against him.

Behind him Silver and Amber and Jade were half blinded by rain and were desperately miserable. There was no shelter anywhere in the world. The night threatened them. Flashes of lightning showed sodden deer huddled together, closing their eyes against the glare, seeking to hide from the wind that savaged them. It was a cold wind, coming from the North, a memory of winter.

Shelter. It was the only thought in the wildcat's mind. But there was no shelter. Pools had collected under the trees; pools had formed in the angling rocks; the cave where her young had been born was hidden in a torrent that drove towards the rapids. The rush of falling water added to the clamour.

It also obscured the sound of tumbling rocks, so that Chia forgot that they were running from the avalanche and turned back, bewildered and distressed, to seek a hiding place higher on the slopes. The main mass of boulder was surging towards the waterfall, an edge of outlying pebbles tumbling after it. One of the larger stones hit Amber on the head.

Silver mewed in terror as he saw his sister fall. Chia turned and saw the small lifeless body lying on the ground. The other kittens watched, bewildered. The last pebbles slid away in a slither of dust. There was grit in Fury's eyes, and he sat and pawed at them forlornly, temporarily blinded. Another pebble bruised Silver's shoulder, and he licked frantically at the hurt, trying to ease the pain. Jade ran to Chia. Chia had eyes only for her dead kitten. She licked the bleeding head and then lifted the warm body with her mouth. She led the way to the edge of the moor and here she and the kittens crouched together, under a bush that showered them with raindrops, enduring the long desolate hours, and Chia kept Amber beneath her as if hoping to warm her to life.

Morning came, sombre clouds sullenly threatening more rain. The wind had lessened. The trees no longer bent to the ground with each fresh gust. The sodden birds huddled in misery. The deer came on to the slope. Chia licked at her dead kitten, aware of the stiffening body, knowing her tongue could never restore movement. She mourned at the sky and Jade crept towards her, pushing against her, tongue busy on her mother's paw, while Silver and Fury watched, bewildered.

It was time to go. Chia waited while the kittens nosed their dead sister, at first puzzled, and then in recognition. She scraped soil over the broken body, and then hissed, and they followed her, and bedded for the day in the shelter of the rocks some way from the mouth of their old den. Chia could not hope to excavate the earth that blocked it. It was useless as a home. That afternoon rain fell once more and the beasts on the hill, and the birds in the trees, and the wildcat and her family crouched forlorn, and could find no warmth. The three little beasts slept fitfully but the wildcat lay wide-eyed, remembering Amber, desolate, sorrowing. Jade, too, was lonely for her sister when she woke.

Evening brought respite. The clouds cracked and the sun shone briefly. The weather changed and a dry warm wind from the South stroked gently over the damaged land. The birds plucked new courage from the air and sang, led by a distant cuckoo.

The warm wind heralded a warm night, lit by a rampant moon that rose big and bold over the edge of the distant mountain.

Light poured on loch and moor and hill and hollow, etching the shadows black and deep. Chia took the kittens hunting, showing them how to move through the darkness, avoiding moonfingers that would point them plain to any marauder. There was always the hooting owl, watching for movement, sitting swivel-headed, unseen, on a branch; the kits must learn caution.

Caution! She hissed it at them and they melted into the shadows, wary, alerted by the thump of rabbit-leg on the ground, by the sharp bark of a startled deer, by the sudden cry from a frightened bird. Caution, she snarled, startling them with her anger, as they rested in the half-light at daybreak, and the eagle, early astir and hungry, threatened above them, looming high. Caution, she warned, as the sudden screech of a hunting hawk struck fear into the dawning and each kit froze against the ground, merging into the backcloth of fern and bramble, whin and tussocky heather. Caution, she mewed softly, as Old Scarface prowled on his errands, unaware that Fergus waited for him at the end of the trail. They no longer tarried. Even Silver was learning fast, and was as quick as the others to hide when his mother told him.

Chia knew her territory intimately. She remembered an abandoned badger's earth, not far from the scene of Old Scarface's kills. It was an astonishing maze of meandering tunnels and she led them to it. The new home entranced the kittens, who explored the dark world deep underground and found the central chamber, musty with age and long untenanted. The rotting bedding held the faint, elusive, long-standing smell of badger.

The earth had last been occupied by an old rogue, a beast that had only two toes on his hind foot, having been caught in a trap and torn himself free. His lameness had been a severe handicap, as the wound festered, and the whole limb shortened. He turned to lambs, and although he stole only those that were newly dead, Fergus dared not trust him, and ended the beast's life as he left the sett one spring evening. No other badger had taken the home. The wildcat family rested, thankful to be dry, and free from the tormenting wind that chilled wet fur and made the world a weary place for a beast without a home.

Some hours later the wildcat led her young from the entrance of her new home for the first time; she caught the scent of man, and hissed them back into the darkness. She herself lurked in the mouth of the sett, looking down. She saw the fox. The kittens crept to peer out beside her, curious.

Fergus had baited the ground. A lamb, its neck broken when it fell over a rockface that afternoon, lay among the boulders near the site of the old fox's first kill. Scarface had come back twice, but Fergus had been prepared for him and twice fired after him, only to have the irritation of seeing a defiant brush wave gaily and vanish. Tonight the keeper was more cunning. He left the dogs at home, to their intense disgust, lest their scent warn the beast. He checked the wind, and lay behind a tumble of rock a few yards above the dead lamb. If only the wind did not change. It had veered once that evening.

It was uncanny, lying alone in the night. He was bereft without a dog at his knee. He was aware of the slightest sound on the air, of the far faint whine of a car changing gear on the hilly road several miles away; of the distant suck of the sea on the shore; of a bat, hawking in the last of twilight, flying within inches of his head and, as it flittered into a tree, its wings flicked against the leaves and branches, reminding Fergus of a child running past a paling fence, flashing at it with a stick. He yawned, weary. He must not doze. Deliberately he blanked out thought and began to count. One hundred, and still no sign of the fox. Perhaps Scarface would not come that night. Perhaps he had fed royally on some beast injured by the storm. Perhaps he had fed on a deer-calf. Two hundred. The moon picked out the shadows, threw ghost leaves, shivering, on the ground, turned tree stumps into hiding beasts and a brooding stag into a tree stump. The bat had gone. Four hundred. Fergus's left knee ached, and he had a pain in his shoulder and the gun was a burden that he longed to set aside.

Five hundred. Five hundred and one. Five hundred and——. There was a sound of padding paws on rock. The dogfox was coming, certain he was alone. He appeared, brush lifted high, running over the crest of a tiny ridge, eager to feed on the lamb that lay dead, announcing its presence on the wind. Wind that had been kind and had not shifted.

Scarface reached the lamb. One sniff was enough and he bent his head and tore at the wool. He had the taste of blood in his mouth when the gun spat fire and he kicked and rolled.

The wildkits were standing in the opening of the sett, motionless but alert. They saw the man stand stiffly, his gun in his hand, and walk over to the beast. The open eyes stared in hatred. The fox was not yet dead. Fergus fired again, standing over the twitching body which kicked and then lay still. The kittens cowered beside their mother, watching closely. They had learned a new lesson. Now they would always fear guns.

The fox carcase was tempting but Chia did not intend to touch it. The smell of the man was too strong. He might have laid a trap for her. The body was suspect. She took the kittens through thick brush to the rabbit warren, and hunted for them until the small mists that heralded dawn warned her it was time to return and sleep.

Fergus felt a thrill of satisfaction. The poacher had died on the hill, had been punished for his faults. A second later, as always, he felt pity for the dead beast. He never enjoyed the act of killing. He left the carcase, and went home. His unease was soothed by a wild welcome from the dogs who vied with one another to greet him and attract his attention.

Later he sat by a hurriedly re-kindled woodfire, stretched in his armchair, Tip on its back occasionally mischievously tweaking his hair. The dogs shared the rug. Tim leaned a head against his knee, Jackie as always lay with his chin on the man's shoe. Fergus yawned. It had been a long day. He stroked the dogs' heads, and planned the morrow, and wondered where next to look for the wildcat.

CHAPTER SEVEN

The kittens needed meat. They were growing fast. They were alert, adventurous, and mischievous, becoming daily more agile. The world beyond their home tempted them, called to them, exciting, tantalising, intriguing, filled with rustles and murmurs that demanded investigation, yet able to turn on them, fear-filled and terror-laden. Chia was exhausting herself, her watchfulness constant. They were so small and inexperienced, and only she could keep them safe. The eagle threatened daily, watching the world beneath him, hoping for an easy kill. The shadow of his wings on the ground sent the kits to immediate cover. They had learned to recognise death.

Death visited them regularly as Chia killed rabbit and leveret and once caught an injured hare, lamed by a cut on his hind paw, made by a sharp end of wire. The cut had festered and the abscess was raw. He lay quiet in his form, pain darkening the sunshine, and only cared for life when the sun was hot on his fur and the heat of its rays eased the hurt. Chia ended his misery and brought him release.

The wildcat was gaunt. Jade and Silver and Fury fought for the meat that she brought them, and often she could not catch enough for all. She began once more to hunt by day, choosing her time, and twice Fergus found his chickens missing. Having wandered on to the moor to lay their eggs in secrecy, under a bush where he would not find them, they did not live to stray again. The kittens revelled in chicken meat.

They were seven weeks old when the wildcat, returning home in the half-light that heralded dawn, having caught nothing all night, heard a deer, its bleat plaintive. She crouched listening, conscious of the terror near by, of desperation in the animal's cries. She was also aware of birds hiding in the bushes. A grouse brooded her chicks under her wing and cowered, panic-stricken, afraid that the little ones might betray their presence. They, knowing her fear, were as still as the grey outcrop boulders that studded the ground.

The wildcat was vividly aware of the scent of the earth beneath her, of the musty decaying leaves lying around her, too wet to rustle when she moved. She was aware of the rough bark of the tree against which she was pressed, using its shadow to hide her presence. She flexed her claws and fanned her ears. Her green eyes searched the wood.

She was in one of the forestry plantations. It was bordered by wire fences to keep the deer from encroaching on the new growth. The wire stretched in front of the wildcat and, as she watched, she saw it tremble. She ran, soft footed, silent as midnight, along the edge of the fence.

The deer was young, a last year's calf. He had tried to jump, and failed, and now lay trapped by wire, agonised by the pain of his broken hindleg. Beyond him, his mother watched, a new-born hind-calf sheltering close. She caught the scent of the wildcat, borne to her on the wind. She had her new baby to protect and within a moment she and the calf were running swiftly, panic-crazy, seeking shelter. The abandoned staggie, his first antlers showing as tiny velvet knobs close against his skull, cried out as the wildcat came towards him.

Chia was ravenous. The deer knew little more. His sight-less eyes stared up at the hovering eagle, who missed nothing that might help him feed his family, and who had been floating over the scene for some time, afraid to stoop through the air, lest he hurt himself against the fence. The deer was temptation. The bird watched as Chia checked her hunger. She could not drag the body free. She fed where she had killed. There was food for the kittens, and she would bring them to the feast when darkness shielded them from watching eyes. It was now almost day. The eagle waited in the sky. The wildcat returned to the earth. Jade was looking for her, seated in the mouth of the hole, and greeted her extravagantly. Chia rolled the kitten over, held her daughter with a firm paw, and washed the kit's face.

Jade protested, trying to wriggle free, and her cries brought Silver from the tunnel. There was no sign of Fury.

Fury had been hungry long before Chia returned. He lay in the central chamber, his brother and sister close beside him. He was aware of every movement they made; of the way Jade snuggled against him and curled her head deep under her forepaws; of Silver twitching as he dreamed.

He was aware of other things, as he was always more alert than the remainder of the litter. He felt the tremor of the ground as a small herd of deer raced downhill from some unknown danger. He recognised the call of the questing owl, and the sudden dying scream of some little beast. The owl had found a baby weasel. The mother heard him too late, and raced home to find only three instead of four kits venturing out of the hole in the bank where she had thought them safe. She mourned until daybreak.

Fury was restless. The night called to him. He longed to taste the darkness, to hunt for himself in the grasses, to find mouse, or chick, or small soft furred rabbit. His paws twitched with excitement, and his heart raced. Saliva trickled from his mouth and he licked his lips.

He left his sleeping brother and sister and crept along the passage that led outside. He was very new to life, and the night-time world, seen for the first time without his mother, on his own, was much bigger and noisier than he expected. He nearly turned back, as the wind chased through the trees and scurried through his fur, and swept tiny eddies of leaves from the ground.

It was an exciting wind, full of news. He knew none of the smells; all were strange and all were enticing. Then faint as the trail of a snail over dry ground came the suggestion of food; a rumour, a hint, a quickening of the senses. He lifted his head and sniffed.

The grouse was the wrong side of the wind. Her scent came to him, and with it the scurryings of the twelve chicks that she sheltered. Fergus had marked her nest days before and hoped she would rear all her brood. Grouse were scarce in his domain, and he cherished them. He brought food for them, and scattered it so that they might feed fat and grow strong before winter flung its bitter challenge. Snowfall and icethrall left many starvelings and many weaklings, and fox and stoat and weasel, owl and hawk and eagle, crow and wildcat did the rest. There was never peace.

Fury had learned to move like a hovering snowflake. His tiny paws did not cause a single tremor in any listening beast. No other creature heard him padding stealthily over the ground. He was too small to trouble the bushes, and the grass stems scarcely dipped to his passing. He was ecstatic, a-tremble with the excitement of his first hunt; the full glory of the grouse smell, harsh and strong, called to him.

It lacked half an hour to full light. The owl, a faraway moan, hunted beside the loch and called to his mate. She, secure on her nest high in a hollow tree, answered him and gentled her downlings, huddled at her feet. A bird woke and sang, a brief note that was silenced when the owl called again. The grouse moved, calling her chicks to her. They were restless and inquisitive, and one, in particular, was too bold for his own good.

He ranged beyond her sight and her quick soft cluck called him back, but he did not hear. He was mesmerised. He was standing in a diminutive clearing, a downy feather-ball of fluff, bright eyed and eager, and he was staring up at an immense, terrifying creature, four-footed, furred. He had never seen anything like it in his brief life. Instinct roused his fear. He crouched, feigning death, immobile, hoping that lack of movement would keep him safe. His action was too late. Fury had fed on chicks before, and had seen this one move and he pounced, and killed. Pride mastered him. He mouthed his catch and slipped softly away, while the grouse cried her lamentations to the sky and the newly-waking birds joined her, mourning with her, warning one another that death walked beneath them, that death had come, four-footed, to the kill.

The chick was a nothing of bone and feather, a mouthful, a momentary satisfaction, but it was first blood and Fury took it to show his mother. Even in his pride, he was cautious, sliding through brambles, well hidden, knowing that eagle watched and hawk waited, that owl hunted in the gloaming and the dawning and that every other creature, on the hill or in the air, brought swift and instant death.

The eagle was irritable. He had torn at the deer carcase,

hoping to free it and take it piecemeal to his nest, but he could not rip enough of the beast away. Others were feeding hungrily as soon as he left. He had fed his single eaglet, and brought food to his mate. She had camouflaged the nest again with more green branches of mountain ash, ripped by her vicious beak from a solitary tree that dug gnarled roots into a rocky ledge and defied the mountain storms that raced along the slopes; storms that twisted and stunted bushes to nightmare freaks and stroked the trees until they lay flat topped, angling against the ground, in shapes that defied reason.

The eagle saw the grasses move gently as Fury slid between them. Chia, anxious, was hunting for her kit, her soft call mewing and plaintive as she sought his trail. He heard her and answered. The chick fell to the ground. He stopped and mouthed it, unwilling to leave his first kill, anxious to show his prowess, and ran unguardedly across the barren shale that led to the tangle of thick sticks and twigs and heather and grass that sheltered the mouth of the sett.

The eagle fell from the sky, the air singing as he stooped. His talons were outstretched, but Chia heard him, sensed him, rather than saw him, and ran, swifter than snakedart, grabbing her son roughly by the loose fur at his neck. Startled, he dropped the hard-won chick, and cried plaintively, urgently desiring his catch, his pride, his trophy. He struggled and Chia bit. There was no time for patience. He relaxed, his faint mew sorrowful. Chia and Fury were well inside the earth when the eagle braked, disappointed. He took the chick and swallowed it, scarcely noticing the titbit. Enraged and hungry, he soared into a sky blue with morning, washed with a glisten of light, and marred by clouds that piled in high pillars over the faraway peaks.

Fury spat, enraged by the theft. Chia licked him, her tongue swift and busy; she had been sure that he was gone for ever and she was delighted to see him. Jade, jealous, bit her brother's paw, and he tore himself free from his mother's caresses and rolled to fight his sister, drawing blood from her ear. She mewed in anger. A moment later, they had forgotten the fight and Fury worried the deer meat that Chia had brought them, dragging it from the carcase. He forgot, for the moment, his own hunt and catch, but the memory lingered.

That night, Chia took the kittens with her when she went hunting. They could no longer be trusted to remain in the earth, and there were too many dangers. She led them through the heather tunnel that followed the fold of the hill, and brought them to the dilapidated old barn. Here Fergus kept a stock of hay on which he could feed the winter-bound sheep and deer and his two Highland cows.

Mice made inroads on the food and not even Dragon, hunting in his waking time, could keep them down. Jackie, accompanied by Bran and Tim, came often to hunt rats and accounted for a good proportion. Bran tried to help, but his amiable bumbling did more harm than good, alerting the vicious brutes to the terrier's presence, and the Labrador tired easily, flopping on the ground, thumping his tail to spur Jackie in his campaign against the vermin that Fergus hated. The keeper would not lay poison so near his house. At times he took the terrier and used his gun, but the war was never-ending and he sometimes thought the rodents had some secret means of communication, so that they could send word far and wide to all their relatives that here was good feeding.

Chia accounted for five rats before they left, and Fury found a small mouse cowering in a corner, played with it, and killed it. Silver tried to take it from him, rousing instant rage. Fury crouched over his prey, his trophy, and lowered his ears and snarled, meaning everything his expression said. Abashed, Silver returned for comfort to his mother, and killed the half-mauled mouse that she brought for him. She watched closely, ready to intervene should he lose the wounded victim, but Silver was inspired by his brother's example, and stalked and patted and tapped, and finally pounced and proudly carried the mouse home with him, having fed well on rat.

Only Jade failed to kill that night, being too afraid of being left alone, so that whenever her mother was busy about her own affairs, the little female shadowed her, and shared her mother's prey. The wildcat tried twice to make Jade hunt an injured mouse but the kitten was timid. The lust to kill was latent in her, as yet undeveloped.

The birds were starting the dawn chorus when Chia led

them home. Both brothers carried a dead mouse. The family stopped in a tiny clearing and drank from a pool. Chia, knowing home was near and dawn only a soft gleam on the horizon, sat on a rock and allowed the kittens to play. They were growing fast, their fur thick, their clubtails bushy. Jade chased Silver's tail, while Fury tossed his mouse in the air and batted at it with an inexpert paw, missing it entirely. He sat to consider the matter. He tried again, and again he missed his target.

He tapped the mouse thoughtfully. It was a dull toy, now that it was dead. The tail did not twitch. The body did not pulse with frightened life. There was no pleasure in it. He tossed it high in the air, stood on his hind paws, and snatched it as it fell. His claws caught in the fur.

This was a better game, a satisfaction that recaptured the thrill of the chase. He tried again, and again he slashed the twisting body out of the air. He mouthed it, and carried it proudly to Chia and leaned against her. She licked his head, and he dropped the dead mouse and purred contentedly.

Jade had been watching her brothers. She had no mouse to carry. She saw Fury sitting with his, unattended, at his feet and crept forward to take it. Instantly he was upon it, daring her to snatch it from him, snarling at her, his expression wicked. She slipped away, defeated.

There was a shrew squeaking in the grasses. She heard him, and crept towards him and stopped, paw lifted, head on one side, intrigued. He moved, and suddenly she too knew the quick lust of the hunt and pounced and killed. Her mew of triumph alerted Chia, who ran towards her daughter to investigate her catch. She saw the kitten mouth the shrew, recognised it, knowing it poison, snatched it and slapped hard at Jade, who cried out, puzzled. Her two brothers, mystified, came to watch. Chia held the shrew in her mouth for a moment, shuddering at the remembered taste and the remembered sickness that had come soon after. She dropped the carcase and spat and snarled. The kittens sniffed at the body. Chia's warning sounded in their ears. They would never taste the bitter flesh or know the hours of pain that followed, but none of them would ever try to eat a shrew again, though they might kill it for practice. Chia buried the carcase. It was found by a mole who unearthed it and ate it, unaffected by the poison.

It was time to go. Already the eagle hunted and the hawk was abroad. The owl had gone to roost. The small sounds of day echoed on the dawn-bright air. The plaintive waking note of a sleepy bird, the reply from its mate, was followed by the sudden call of a cuckoo, bell-like. The cooing of pigeons, far away in the wood, was clearly audible to the wildcat. She recollected the taste of pigeon and her mouth watered.

The weasel ran past, her body undulant in the grass. Fury heard her first and his quick hiss alerted his mother. She called the kits and they crouched beside her. The weasel had other thoughts in her head. She was returning to the carcase of a deer that had died on the mountain. It had been shot by a careless poaching gun, and limped in agony for weeks. The never-healed flesh was gangrenous, and the beast too weak to feed. Death came, merciful, at last. On her way to the hill the weasel slipped in and out of a rabbit burrow and emptied it of young. The rank scent lay there for the doe to recognise and she was mourning, sorrow brooding on the air as she discovered her ravished nest.

The eagle saw the weasel as she ran along the path between the heather tussocks, returning to the dead deer. She used the trail daily and he had seen her before. He plotted her path and, as she reached the bare ground and turned towards her target, his wings clipped the air and the thump of his body as he landed broke her back. Within minutes she was tossed among the mountain ash, on the vast raft-like nest high on the bare rocky ledge, and the young eagle, who had screamed a demanding welcome, was tearing the meat. Three weasel kits were left motherless, and died when the wildcat caught them as they hunted inexpertly, starving for food.

The eagle soared into the sky. He saw the deer lying where the weasel had found it. A fox was tearing at the flesh. Hoodie crows waited in the bushes. The eagle watched.

Fergus, walking with his gun, was noting the grouse nests and marking the new deer-calves with ear tags, so that he could take part in a scheme which registered as many new-born deer as possible, their weights, their sex, their territory, and the length of their lives. He saw the eagle and wondered. The bird was obviously watching something on the ground below. Then he noticed a hind, head drooped, standing in the bushes. He could not see the dead deer or the feeding fox, both hidden behind a rise in the ground. He motioned the dogs to instant rest, then took his spyglass and focused on the beast. A huge swelling marred one shoulder. There were signs of botfly infestation in her nostrils, and her ribs were stark lines against her mangy fur. He put down the spyglass and lifted his rifle and sighted carefully. She was outlined perfectly, the crossed lines centring on her heart. He fired. She dropped, her misery ended.

Fergus, examining her, discovered that the swelling lay above a wound caused by a bullet. There had been raiders on the hill. The injury was not more than six weeks old. He had heard nothing and seen nothing, but there were two stags that had vanished from the further glen where both had hidden while in velvet. He thought that the storm might have frightened them into deeper sanctuary. Now he wondered. Probably the men he had caught were responsible. They had known the ground. He sighed, wishing he had help. It was difficult for one man alone to police so much territory.

There was always a market for illicit venison. He had not watched carefully enough. He left the hind, and crested the rise. The fox heard him and ran. The crows flapped away heavily. He stared down at the dead deer, noting its injuries. There had indeed been two-legged predators armed with guns.

Fergus was a conscientious man, a dedicated man, and the neglect fretted him. They must have come while he was busy with the lambing. The men he caught, who had now been tried and heavily fined, must have made a previous sortie. It was an irritating thought, but at least if they were responsible, they had paid for their folly. The fines had been vicious. He looked down at the dead hind. He recognised her. She had lost a calf in a peat bog the year before. She might forget faster than man, but beasts suffered pain and fear, they sheltered their young, they felt grief at their death. Was man, in his arrogance, any wiser or any better? He pondered the pitiful carcases. He hated taking life from anything but the rats and beasts that, like the fox and the wildcat, preyed on his livestock. Yet, even with them, he knew remorse, as he found them beautiful. The fox, running free over the moor, was a splendid creature and the wildcat, though he hated her for her depredations, was magnificent.

Man was strange, the keeper thought as he walked back to the house to make breakfast. He bred beasts for market, and knowing their end, still spent his time and care on them, grew fond of them, and hated to see them go. Fergus always enjoyed lambing time, enjoyed watching the small creatures learn to live and leap, and hated the day on which the big truck came and took them away, feeling that he had betrayed them.

It was absurd, yet he never shot grouse or pheasant without feeling pity as he lifted the lifeless creature, and saw light die from its eyes and life fade from the feathers. Even a fish taken from the water, lost its grace and was a pathetic thing. Often, watching the leaping salmon climb the ladder to find the spawning grounds, he found himself sympathising with them, and later was reluctant to cast his fly. When he did so, the struggle to land his catch enthralled him, and pride and sadness mingled when the splendid silver body lay defenceless on the bank. It was difficult at times to understand his own nature, or to reconcile his hunting with his pity for the kill.

He walked thoughtfully up the hill, the dogs shadowing him. The day was warm, and his flapping coat enlarged him, giving him a wild appearance so that the kittens, watching him from their secret cover, having seen the hind die, saw his winged outline, reminiscent of the eagle, and crept towards one another, trembling. Chia crouched above them, desperately afraid. The dogs knew they were there and Tim growled a warning, but Fergus was hungry and had spent too much time already and had other jobs waiting. He whistled the Labrador to heel.

Chia waited until they had gone. It was necessary to cross their trail to reach the earth where the wildcats lay during the day. It was warm and she would have liked to bask in the sun, but the scent was rank and lingered; the ground that they had bruised, reeked, and alarmed her. She hissed at the kits and they sped, taking a devious route, seeking safety, buried deep in the dark cold earth.

More than an hour passed before they forgot the smell of the man and his accompanying dogs, and even then the thick fur on Fury's tail still bristled and Silver dreamed of giant paws that thundered towards him, and he mewed, woke, and huddled close against his mother, striving to recapture remembered comfort from her now almost-dry teats. Jade, lying between the wildcat's front paws, felt safe and relaxed and her small breathy purr enlivened the darkness.

A mole, blundering into the tunnel from one of his own workings, which had given way, smelled the cat family and fled, pell-mell, in blind panic. None of the wildcats caught his scent and he escaped, and dived beneath another of his runs, and fed avidly on earthworms to solace himself after his fright.

Outside the sett death waited, disguised in many forms, and the bright sun spilled its bounty on the earth, and the deer basked in the rare warm air. Fergus, tempted by the brilliance, watched the dogs swimming in the pool beneath the waterfall and joined them, briefly, wondering how many years had passed since last he dived into the sheer green deeps and revelled in such sunshine.

CHAPTER EIGHT

The kittens were learning fast. Chia taught them daily. Taught them to watch, to crouch, to freeze at the hint of a sound; to hunt, to pounce, to kill. She took them past the rocky crevice where the polecats hid, and stood sniffing the wind. The kittens mimicked her, each in a characteristic pose. Jade stood close beside her mother, almost between her forepaws, so that Chia had to take care when she jumped. Fury stood aloof, snarling, his whole body one ferocious implicit threat. His ears lay flat on his head. Silver always waited with his small head cocked inquisitively, one forepaw lifted and curled, his eyes imbued with intense curiosity.

One well-remembered night, when the kits were nine weeks old and June was fading in midsummer heat, Silver was first from the earth. He sniffed, and was immediately drenched in the taint that came out of the ground, was borne on the breeze, and filled his nostrils. It was fear-stink, terror-stink, stink recognised immediately, known for generations, the stink of the little brutes that brought quick death to the unweary, that vied for food, that fed on the sleek bodies of the other creatures that hid on the hill. There was no defence and no latitude for the very young when the little snake-swift killers struck. Silver's fur bristled. It was a smell he would never forget as long as he lived, and his own intuition was reinforced by his mother's stance, telling him it was a smell to heed and to fly from.

Fury trusted nothing. Long before he caught the rank tang and identified it he was ready to fight, ears flattened and lips drawn back, ferocity embodied in miniature. He hissed and spat, and backed away. There was a polecat family in the crack that led to a small, weatherproof cave.

Four half-grown young lay with their mother and added to their own body taint was the stench from the half-eaten carcases that lay near by. The polecats killed for fun, taking far more than they needed.

Jade, as always, was timid and stood close beside her mother, pressing against the wildcat's hindleg, needing her caress. The smell and the sounds that came from the crack terrified her and she trembled, and her heart raced frighteningly. Chia licked the little head and called the kittens on. They slipped past stealthily, anxious to avoid attention.

The wildcat showed them the hidden ways through tussock and bramble. She taught them how to avoid the boggy patches, and how to recognise them by the quake and tremble of the soaking moss, by the water that started between their paws, by the shiver in the ground when weight, however slight, was allowed to rest on the tummocks. She took them round the edges of the gulping peat-hags, where big stags could wallow in safety, but where a small kit could trap and drown. She led them through intriguing rocky gullies, where a man could stride waist deep and see all around him, but where, for them, cliffs loomed high and challenged the kittens to climb. They struggled upwards, clawing at the grey grass that cloaked the ledges, while Chia leaped lightly, and watched from above, intent on the world around her, as well as on the progress of her young.

Instinct sharpened her wits, so that she knew, without seeing, when the eagle shadowed the hill; was aware of deer browsing beyond her; was alert for the slide of weasel or slip of stoat through tussocky grass that was harsh and tangled with dead winter growth. She did not need eyes to warn her of the sparrowhawk. She needed the instinct that told wild creatures of danger, that read the throbbing air, that interpreted the news on the wind.

Should any creature threaten her young, electric impulses spread pricklingly over her skin, rousing each separate hair of her fur; ears flattened, she turned, at bay. An unwary questing beast, seeing her, never stayed to challenge but fled, feeling behind it the hot breath of the pursuer, closer in imagination than in reality.

The hill was Chia's domain; the ground as far as the wire deer fence on one side and beyond it on the other; the lower slopes that led to the rippling burn; the land that slid away to contain Fergus's house. There, in the garden, Dragon was supreme and Chia did not challenge him. Nor did he do more than swear at her. At night she was careful only to visit when he was away from home. Lying hidden in the tree, she saw him set off towards the moor, where he could hunt and eat, and savour the night. Dragon was old and wise, and did not care to fight. He preferred to bask by the fire or lie in the sun, and catch little creatures that could not threaten him.

Life was total experience, intense, with death only a heart beat away. Chia watched anxiously as the kittens stalked the grasses. She saw Fury play with a butterfly and slash it from the sky as he leaped. For the first time he gained instant satisfaction from a skilful movement that rewarded his judgement, although the crushed butterfly was useless and uneatable. Unless he learned to strike and kill he would starve when on his own, and time was passing.

There was much to do and little time for lessons. Urgency mastered Chia. She caught the sheltering mice and brought them to the kits alive and supervised their killing. She found the trail of grouse chicks and showed the kits where the feather balls were hidden. One early dawn six small forepaws wrought disaster in the wood, and the grouse herself, mourning, was caught by Chia who ate from a toss of feathers, growling softly whenever any of the kits came near. Even Jade was forced to wait till her mother had sated her hunger.

The sun had strengthened to high summer. When hunting was done the wildcats curled together in a secret patch where the rays fell against rock and soothed their fur. They lay basking in the rare warmth, ecstatic, tempting the eagle, who looked for one alone, but not for four; Chia never relaxed her guard.

The kits teased one another and teased the grasses and tapped at Chia's whiskers until she hissed them to be still. They were fifty times as lively as they had been only the week before, were alert, were kitten-curious, needing to hunt down the squeak in the scrub, or chase a shadow that streamed across the grass, or to try and tap the twitching leaves from the branches.

There was enticement in the slither of a straw over the ground, in the dance and whirl of a leaf tossed by the wind; in the sudden flight of a small bird from tree to bush to bramble twig. There was entrancement in the shifting, running, rippling, glinting water, bubbling in the shallows, shining in the sunlight, alive with darting minnows. The kittens dipped their paws, trying to catch the spinning glitter, puzzled by reflections that seemed so real, but that eluded them, time and again.

The water tossed small trophies to the shore. A dead fish made a brief plaything as Fury tapped its tail and the fins flickered. Bubbles in the pool, from a young otter questing down stream, were a sight for marvelling, and the kittens danced along the bank watching the strange movement in the water. When the sleek wet head surfaced briefly, and the dog otter looked at the world with merry bright eyes, the kittens vanished and were no more than a brief memory for the little beast that dived again, and was gone. It was ten minutes before Chia found them, lying together, fur ruffled, trembling, and her quiet tongue licked them and told them that all was well.

She had left them briefly as she went to hunt mice in the early glim of morning. The otter, coming home, had disturbed her and, seeing his sleek back as he dived, she pondered catching him, but desisted. He would not land near her and she did not care for swimming. And he would fight furiously. She turned and, missing the kittens, tracked them swiftly, following their trail with her nose, listening for their betraying sounds with quick ears that were never at fault. She was delighted to find them safe and they greeted her extravagantly, Silver and Fury dancing at her and tapping her whiskers, and Jade holding her mother's muzzle tightly with both front paws and licking at her furred face. Chia purred to them and they answered her, the air thrilling to the sound so that a chaffinch, high in the tree above, heard them and yelled a warning, and birdcalls echoed around them. It was not safe to linger. Man might come, trying to divine the reason for the noise, and man meant death.

A moment later the shadows had swallowed them. It was not yet time for bed. They were fed and merry with mischief. Fury saw a squirrel high in a tree. The branches were broken ruins, only the tips alive, dark with dense green needles. The squirrel was leaping swiftly along the topmost branch in order to jump to another tree that offered more cover. A sparrowhawk loomed in the sky and might be able to snatch him from the bare perch. He needed protection.

Fury climbed the tree, his needle-like claws gripping tightly. He had never climbed so high before, and he forgot all caution as he sped towards the squirrel, not knowing that he could not hope to catch it, nor that he could not pounce or spring when he was anchored tightly and he dared not let go. The squirrel saw him, chattered a furious warning, and jumped to safety. Fury, disappointed, looked down. Far below him, incredibly dwarfed, he saw his brother and sister. Chia was watching him, sitting on a log that lay across the clearing, her head cocked, her eyes interested.

It was a very long way to the ground. He lost his confidence, and slipped, and fell several feet before his claws gripped again. He clung to the rough bark, desperately frightened, feeling it harsh against the bare black skin of his pads, afraid that the wind thrusting against his fur might blow him away, as it blew the twisting leaves. A sudden gust shook his perch and he mewed loudly, terrified. He was not safe, the ground was so far away, and he was so very small and very lonely. He needed his mother. He dared not climb down. He did not know how to turn round. He might fall. The wind seethed through the dry branches and the tree creaked horrifyingly. Fury wailed.

Chia ran to the tree. She climbed swiftly, expertly, knowing how to anchor her claws, knowing where to put her weight. She reached her son and gripped him in her jaws. She did not attempt to turn but came down backwards, clinging tightly, paws around the trunk, the kitten limply dangling from her mouth. She was afraid that the tree was sighing its death song, was about to fall. She also felt unsafe. She was almost on the ground when a tremendous gust, blowing up from nowhere, pushed the tree to its limit and she jumped the last few feet and fled, to cower with the other kittens under a bush. The tree groaned as it heaved from the earth. The ground shook. Frightened small beasts dived out of cover and ran headlong, among them an old grouse lame from an unskilled shot. The wildcat could not resist the limping bird. Soon she and the kittens lay among the feathers and slept off their meal, though Fury and Chia only dozed, conscious of every sound that echoed, from the sigh and stir of the wind between gusts to the flail and rip of the branches when it strengthened, and the cheep and twitter and call of the birds busy about the day's happenings.

They slept till the sun flung cool shadows across them and clouds chilled the air, and then made their way along the hidden paths to the sett. Fury dug briefly and uncovered a dead mouse which Chia had buried. He carried it inside, wanting only to play. He did not like the taste of carrion. He tapped at it, but he was weary and finally left it. The sleep that overtook the four of them lasted until the bats flicked out of the trees to quarter the air for insects.

The sun was setting in a sky sliced with scarlet streamers. The clouds behind were black, edged with gold. Light streamed on to the hill, cascading in a golden glow that picked out tree and bush and a lolloping hare too far away to consider. The wildcat sought to read the wind; nothing threatened her. She mewed and the kittens came out, tumbling over one another, heady with excitement.

There was excitement in the wind; in the insects that raced over the ground; in a scurry from the grass, where a shrew fled in horror, seeing Silver loom near him. Silver was chasing Fury's tail, wanting to grapple in mock fight, and the two kittens soon sprawled in a twist of thrashing paws and flailing tails, until Fury lost his temper and yowled in anger, and bit his brother's ear. Silver did not want to prolong the fight. He rolled free, and sat and shook his head.

Fury jumped to a small rock and looked around him. There was an old stump left from a tree long forgotten, and he sharpened his claws, stretching languorously, revelling in the sensation that he experienced as he ripped away the bark. The trunk was scored by Chia and her kittens.

Darkness came. The half-moon crept up the sky, hanging above the shining water. The bats vanished. A chill wind crept out of the North and rippled the pools. Waves on the shore of the sea loch soughed on the quiet air. Nature lay brooding. An owl flew, swift and silent, brushing the bushes, questing for food.

The kittens sat, immobile, an inner tremble of delight dominating each small body, as they waited for mouse squeak or the unwary soft thump of a small rabbit or leveret, playing under the stars.

The wind was a murmur, a whisper, a faint touch on the fur, scarcely shivering the leaves. A fox yelped, startling the dark. A deer, shifting on its bracken bed, rustled the undergrowth and then snorted. It was a full-grown stag, wide-browed, with antlers covered in velvet. When they were full-grown he would dominate the hill, imperious. Just now he wanted quiet, and lived alone, waiting for the savage excitement of the rut to call him to find his hinds and choose his harem.

Chia ignored him. He was too big to fight and kill. The kittens knew he was there. They now knew deer smell and weasel smell, could recognise the bird tang that lay on the ground where the grouse sheltered their chicks; they knew mouse smell and shrew smell and that of the tunnelling mole; they knew, and feared above all, the smell of man, and his dogs. They knew about guns. They knew the safe retreats through bracken and bramble, the twist of a gully, the lie of a ditch, the ways that led through deep cover back to their earth. They were learning fast, and each day was a bonus, snatched from eternity. Each day ensured new knowledge. Chia, watching them, her eyes serene, purred contentedly and nuzzled each adoringly, revelling in her young.

There was a flash of movement. A buck rabbit, scudding through the moonlight, scented cat and leaped sideways, driven by terror. He was running blindly and did not see the tawny creatures lying in the dapples made by the moon on grass. He ran, his white scut bobbing, his hindlegs thumping hard as he leaped. Chia was translated in an instant, racing behind him until she was close enough to begin her stalk, so that the rabbit, mesmerised by terror, turned suddenly in a wild attempt to elude her, and jumped towards her instead of away, startling her so much by his unexpected manoeuvre that she failed to twist fast enough and he gained ground.

Fury chased after him. The rabbit was as big as the kitten but Fury did not care. He liked rabbit. He remembered the satisfying warm, tasty flesh and the feel of fur against his teeth. He was almost on the beast. He leaped and clung, his claws raking into the softness below the ribs. The rabbit screamed. Chia, racing swiftly towards the scene, saw his unavailing struggles as he tried to dislodge the demon that was attacking him. She crept forward and pounced, and the rabbit died. Fury, looking up at his mother, snarled at her, telling her that this was his, and he, alone, had killed it. She hissed back at him and he hushed at once. Soon all the family were feeding.

They hunted all night, finding mice and moles, and several chicks. The grouse young had grown and made a more satisfying meal. Between whiles they played, jumping and climbing, teasing and fighting, investigating the small sounds in the grass. Fury played with a grasshopper, intrigued by its leaps. Silver found a frog, wandering some yards from the burn, and patted it, watching it jump. He was no longer hungry and had no desire to kill. The beast leaped senselessly away from the maddening paw that touched it gently, bringing fear of a death that never came. Long after Silver had forgotten it, the frog crouched under a broad leaf, shaking with fright, panting abominably, not daring to move lest the clawed giant paw reached towards it again and brought it back as it fled.

The nights were long; the moon was bright, and there was all the world to explore. Excitement mounted with each new lesson learned and each new kill. The kittens were ten weeks old when summer flared to blossom. The air was rich with flower scent. Yellow flowers starred the furze, harebells grew on the hillside and the kittens played with the bells, watching them bend and bow, curling a paw round the stem, bringing the blue petals down to the ground and releasing them so that they sprang back, to be caught again.

Time was endless. They knew nothing of days and weeks and months, only of daytime and night-time; of flower-time, of warmth and cold, of the wind that brushed the treetops and drove the clouds and creaked the tree trunks; of the waves that splashed on the never-visited beach, a constant mystification that was not questioned.

Their world was of scent that lay close on the ground and hung in the air, that filled their nostrils and told them of hidden creatures ready to assuage their hunger. It was a world where water streamed from the sky, wetting fur and grass and ground; where, sometimes, terror flashed across the clouds and light zigged towards the trees so that one died, struck by the unseen beast, died in a clap of sound that made all other deaths insignificant. It was a world of noise: cheep and squeak and hoot and twitter; snarl and growl and thump and rustle; slide and slither and pad and pant; creak and groan and scream of torment. These things Chia knew, and recognised, and taught them, giving them time; time to grow; time to breed, before lives that were all too brief were ended.

She curled with them, guarding them. Her ears and her nose were their protection. Her claws brought them nourishment. Her speed and wisdom ensured that they too lived to challenge the hill. She lay in the dark and purred. Each movement was reassurance, and she licked Silver as he curled against her, and gentled Jade when she crept close and her paw lay across Fury who was swearing softly as he slept, seeing pictures in his dreams.

CHAPTER NINE

At the beginning of his eleventh week Fury was stalking a beetle in the brightness of dawn. He had no intention of eating it. He had fed, satisfyingly, on mice and a young rabbit and was now playing. The beetle scurried away from him into the grass, and he sat, baffled, a puzzled expression on his face, trying to discover it again. It moved intriguingly, and he enjoyed listening to the rustle of its horny feet on the ground.

He was full-fed and less wary than usual. He was a-thrill with vigour, and leaped high out of the grass for no reason at all, landing on a young nettle shoot. The sharp prick and sting shocked him into caution. He stared at it, bewildered that a mere plant should have power to hurt, and then sat and licked at the smarting pad, and mewed forlornly.

Chia, hearing him, roused herself at once. She was sprawled over the rock, watching Jade and Silver struggle together in mock battle, scrambling over one another, twisting and turning in a flail of paws and tails, nibbling at ears or noses.

The eagle, high above them, saw Fury. His quick brain computed time, space and distance in a lightning calculation, aided by experience and instinct. He noted the mother wildcat, several yards away, and the oblivious tumbling kits. Isolated, tempting, not noticing his surroundings, Fury licked at his sore pad.

The eagle had caught nothing for twenty-four hours. His hunger was a mounting torment, a raging necessity, shouting for a victim. The bird plunged downwards, his shadow speeding towards the ground, the air beating a protest behind him. The wildcat heard, identified, and leaped, her quick brain reacting at once, not a moment needed to reflect or ponder her action. When the eagle braked, the cat was standing above her kitten, enlarged beyond belief, and as he checked and swooped across her, her paw raked at his breast and a spill of blood and feathers stained her fur.

The eagle screamed his rage. Frustration drove him to turn and slash with his talons, although he knew that she could outmatch him. His claws sliced at her head, but she ducked aside and they barely tore the skin. A thin trickle of her own blood mingled with his, and she swore ferociously at him as he turned away, baffled and hungrier than ever, and climbed slowly, his shadow terrifying the hidden beasts that lurked in den and form and hollow, in nest and bush; that pressed, aching with terror, against tree-trunk and sheltering rock, and among tangled roots.

The bird could hear his fledgling screaming for food, and he had none to offer.

Fury was trembling. Chia cuffed him angrily and hissed at him. He should have watched the sky. Forlorn, his pad on fire with the needle pricks of the nettle, he limped behind her, and she called to the other kits and took them to the earth. Day was upon them and she was tired. She could relax deep in the ground. There would be no peace while the eagle was hungry.

There was no peace. The eagle circled the sheep, looking for weak lambs, but Fergus was on the hill with his gun and he released a shot into the air to scare the bird away. The heavy flapping wings lifted the hunter high. He floated on the thermals, watching the hill.

A young hind had borne her first calf. It lay in the bracken, a late-comer to the hill. She had chosen an uneasy resting place and the small head was unprotected. It bleated to her. She was feeding some yards away, the herd behind her. The lead hind barked a warning as death soared over the glen. Startled, the hind turned her head but she was too late. The eagle had chosen wisely, and reckoned his speed and her distance accurately, and the calf died as he hit it. It was difficult to rise into the air. The limp weight hampered him. The hind, moaning eerily, raced towards him, lifted on her hindlegs, and boxed at his body. He was hampered by the weight of the calf. He dropped it, frustrated, knowing he could not rise with such heavy prey. The flailing forehoof struck the edge of the wing and broke three feathers. The bird soared away, angered.

The bleating of the desolate hind worried all the creatures that heard her, and Chia cuddled her three kits closer, knowing that the eagle had found a victim, that another mother hungered for her lost young, and that the kittens were not secure. There was no safety. Even she was not proof against the fiery gun. She remembered her lost daughters and licked urgently at each furred head, and the kits basked in her caresses and their purrs throbbed in the dark. Later, when the hind had abandoned the calf, fox and stoat and polecat fed.

The wind howled all day and blew itself to a standstill just before dusk. The trees, freed from its outraged breath, sighed softly. Rain ceased, and though leaves dripped mournfully, small patters and flurries falling on the saturated ground, there was ease among the beasts.

Mice darted through the grass, their passage bending the stems, small rustles and stifled furtive movements alerting the wildkits who, intensely curious about the world that they had inherited, were growing bold. Chia exhausted herself guarding them.

Fury could climb most trees and descend safely, having learned to master the art. Silver followed more cautiously. Twice he slipped and fell, but both times landed safely, thumping on to all four feet in soft grass at the roots of the big trunk that had tempted him.

Jade only climbed the smaller trees. She was hesitant, slower than her brothers to learn a new skill. She could now recognise mouse snorts and snuffles, knew the way the grass moved as they passed in its unseen deeps, knew the sharp sour-sweet smell that tainted the ground where they scurried, knew what lay inside the grassy nests that rested, domed and hidden, on the ground. She hunted eagerly.

Rabbit daunted her. The fear thump of warning alarmed her as much as it alarmed the rabbits and sent her skeltering to safety, close by her mother's side. Each time Chia comforted her daughter and they moved on to the next warren, but here again the vibrant alarm sent Jade headlong into cover. Silver and Fury learned to disregard the signal, learned to watch for the little one that had not heeded, the rabbitling that continued to play in moonlight or dawnlight, and only knew too late that he had staked his life unwittingly, and lost.

Fury, moving swifter than hawk swoop, three days after the eleventh week of his life ended, had caught a young leveret that beat at him with hard hindlegs and bruised him sorely before he triumphed. He mouthed it proudly, showing it to Chia, who let him keep it for himself, and only when he was filled and content did he allow Jade and Silver to share his catch.

By now they knew the darktime well; they knew the thread of sound from whispering owlwings, the skim of the bird as he swooped low on his kill; they knew the pad, pad, pad, of the loping fox and the rank musk that lay on the air when he scented his territory; they knew the careless tramp and rustle of the old badger, heavy, unafraid, hunting for worm and beetle and slug; they knew the sudden flight of a startled deer and the pant and snort of the stags that lay under trees or flattened soft bracken beds with their large bodies. They knew where the roe-deer hid their kids.

Chia took the family hunting as soon as the rain had stopped. The last faint squalls of wind drove them to frequent shelter, afraid of the noise, uncertain, sure it portended danger. Only when the rustle in the leaves died away did they venture out again, so that their hunting was a series of short forays, and was unrewarded.

Fury, leaping over a fallen log, to land on soft turf, paused, listening. He was excitement embodied, his heart beating a quick tattoo of jubilation as he heard the rustle of a beast moving among leaves that lay, blown and disregarded, in a deep hollow in the ground.

The smell that came from the hollow was new to him. It was food smell, flesh smell, beast smell. It was throat-tightening, saliva-forming, stomach-tingling, speaking to him of warm, newly slain meat, of blood running to sate his appetite; it was an intoxicating smell that tensed his small body, an exhilarating smell that galvanised him to action, an incitement to kill.

He knew better than to hurry. He had learned to control impatience, to master himself so that the stalk was slow, stealthy, a gentle creep, close-furled against the ground, step by tentative step, taking care not to ruffle the grasses, not to tread unwarily on leaves that might crackle, not to give himself away through lack of caution. It was a gentle progression, a murmur of movement, a slither, snake-like, paw by paw; step, and look, and listen, and wait; an extension of slow motion, a drift, a delusion. Any watching beast could scarcely see that the kit had shifted. Fury crept on. The rustling continued, loud, incautious, the noise of an animal that was senseless, stupid, clumsy, unwary, not knowing that murder slid towards him on ink-black pads, eyes glowing with life, teeth bared to bite, paws lanced to kill.

The creature moved again. Fury saw it and stopped in mid-stalk, astounded. He hissed, alarmed beyond reason. He had seen nothing like this in all his life. He glanced anxiously over his shoulder, but Chia and his brother and sister were out of sight, hidden by the log. There was no help there.

At the sound of the hiss the beast stopped and curled itself into a ball. Fury approached curiously, driven by the need for food, by the enticing smell, and by the weird object that lay in his path. He sniffed, and the creature rolled. The wildcat was pricked beyond endurance. He fled to his mother, crying his hurt. The thing had stings in its fur. It had damaged him abominably. His nose hurt and there were specks of blood where he had cleaned it with his paw. His eyes smarted.

Chia leaped the log, anxious to protect her kit. She saw the creature that lay on the path, and stood and called to the other kits. Silver and Fury dashed round the log, skittish and merry, chasing one another, and fell in a teasing tumble in front of the wildcat. She, wishing to teach them, hissed and slapped at the two intertwined bodies with her paw. They disentangled themselves and looked at her.

She led the way to the mysterious creature that lay on the path. Silver approached, it, put out a paw, and retreated, licking his pad. Jade saw his action and was more cautious. The thing smelled like food but it seemed headless and tailless and, moreover, judging by her brothers' behaviour and her mother's warning, it could hurt. She memorised it, and forgot it for the time being and ran at Silver, wanting to play. Wind stirred her coat and excited her. Silver chased her. Chia jumped on to the log and sat above them, listening and watching and reading the wind. Fury clambered up beside her. He had thrust hard and his nose still hurt. He licked his furry leg and pawed at it so that the dampness helped to soothe the pain. Chia turned to him, and her tongue comforted his sorrow.

Behind them, the hedgehog unwound itself and lumbered away. They heard it go. Fury turned to watch. He no longer desired to chase. Silver and Jade played together, leaping and dancing, stalking and tumbling, in a flash of paws and flurry of movement, heady with excitement and a-thrill with life. Fury watched day flush the horizon, and stored in his brain the memory of the beast that walked like food and smelled like food, but had stings in its fur and was, in future, to be avoided.

Dawn brought birdcalls to the hill. The cooings and twitterings were torment to the kits, who listened and hungered and ran to and fro, paws trying to slap the wings from the sky. Only when the eagle's shadow darkened the grass did they desist. Chia called them home. Even then they would not hurry. Fury ran for cover, but Jade patted at the grass stem and Silver played with a feather.

The eagle was weary. He had hunted for weeks, bringing food to the ever-ravenous eaglet, now almost full fledged, that screamed persistently for larger and larger prey. The ledge around the nest was littered with the bones of grouse and grouse chicks, of three fox cubs from three different families, caught over ten days. All had played unwarily. Rabbit and young roe-kid had also gone, new-born, to fill the gaping maw. Three dead lambs further swelled the larder, and a red-deer calf found stillborn was taken piece-meal to feed the eaglet.

On the far side of the eagle's territory the osprey had his home, a nest that had not been found by those who sought to mark the sites, as the bird was rare. His task was simpler than the eagle's as he fed his young on fish and his frequent dive and splash was never unrewarded. His quick eyes noted the swift shape that ruffled the water or fled beneath the waves. He knew the eagle, but both birds observed a strict territorial rule and neither encroached. They did not vie for food.

When dawn was a memory and day gilded the clouds, the eagle saw a movement in the grass below. He split the protesting air, his giant body hurtling down. His talons caught fur; his onslaught snapped the little beast's back.

Silver had not retired to the darkness of the den. He was alert, alive, frisky with youth, wanting to chase his feather as it danced through the grasses. The feather twisted and teased, and he forgot to watch the sky for danger. He heard the roar as the eagle plunged, looked up, and was paralysed by terror. He was too frightened to jump aside, to thrust with armed claws, to snap and snarl and bite. He died as the bird hit him.

Chia, who had been calling desperately, ran. Her claw raked the eagle. He, hampered by the kit that dangled from his talons, was at a disadvantage. He did not intend to abandon his kill. Chia's paw slashed his side, scarring deep. His wings thrust against the air. He had no desire to fight. He rose above her head and ponderously, his wounded side smarting, he flew to the nest and dropped the kit to the greedy beak that worried and ripped and tore.

Jade and Fury had watched from the mouth of the den. They did not need Chia's slap or her urgent hiss to drive them inside. They lay together, trembling. For the rest of the day, if they attempted to move her paw restrained them. She gazed into the darkness, forlorn. The mother-tie was strong; her kits were her world and she had lost three of them. The other two would be even better guarded. She curled herself protectively round them. Jade, as always, tucked beneath her chin. The wildcat dropped her head and at once the affectionate nose met hers, the little tongue leaped to soothe her mother's fur and the tiny beast gave a tremulous purr.

Both kits had seen Silver die. He was Jade's favourite, her playmate. Fury was independent, inquisitive, wary, hunting alone and playing with shadows, a poor companion. He slept but the memory of the eagle marred his dreams, and fear plunged from the sky and the air roared, and Silver died again in a flurry of wings and a terror of noise. Fury woke, trembling, and burrowed into Chia's fur, looking for comfort. He found a dry teat and sucked, and she licked his soft head, knowing his need.

The sun blazed on the hill, flinging wild shadows as birds flew and trees moved in the wind, and grasses bent and swayed. Chia was aware of the heat above and longed to bask in a grassy hollow, but she dared not risk the kits. The eagle had taught her a further lesson.

He, angling hungrily through the air, saw a grouse and soon there were twelve motherless chicks in the wood. Fergus found them at the end of the day and took them back in his cap for his hens to mother. Old Biddy would foster anything that was given to her.

Fed and warmed by the midday heat, the eagle perched on a rock near the nest and preened himself, shining each feather with oil until it lay sleek and smooth against his body. His savaged side was on fire with pain, but in spite of that he had bathed in the early morning. Clean, his plumage immaculate, his belly comfortable, he lazed in the sun, enjoying rare freedom. His mate kept constant watch and the eaglet dozed too. Soon she would fly and the father would be freed from his duties. There would be three hungry shadows haunting the hill.

CHAPTER TEN

Chia no longer needed to warn the kittens to obey her instantly. They both missed Silver, and raced from the shadows that sped over the ground, betraying hawk or owl or eagle. Vigilance was their watchword. Ssss, from a kit and all three were instantly in deep cover. A chak from an alert bird, the sound of deer running, the thud of an alarmed rabbit, needed no reinforcement from their mother. Terror had left deep scars, and was a constant companion.

Stalk and prowl and flash into hiding, never mind food, as life was more important. Creep, and watch, and freeze, never flicking an ear or a whisker, holding breath back until the holding was painful, never twitching a paw or moving an eyelid. Relaxation after the threat had vanished was bliss, was ecstasy, was stretching and rolling, acutely aware of sun warm on thick fur; of wind blowing, stroking from nosetip to tailtip, bringing rumours of other beasts near; of sea-wrack and sea-mist, of rotting weed along the far beaches; of flower-scent, irritating and pungent, the pollen masking small noses, forcing a betraying sneeze.

Life for Jade and Fury was all sensation. The texture of the ground beneath their naked paws spoke to them of mud, which they disliked, or water, which they hated; of crumbly dry earth, in which they could dig easily and bury anything that they had killed and did not wish to eat; of bog, treacherous, sucking at their paws: so that they learned to test the ground before they trod it. They learned the feel of plants, avoiding the sting of nettle, and the needle prick of thistle, loving the rare springiness of the few patches of turf, dodging the claw of bramble.

They learned the easement of green grass when they had

fed too full, and they knew that the water was salt near the loch which was their farthest boundary. They had never explored the beach. Chia was afraid of the tides, which held a mystery she could not solve, so that one day the beach was bare and on another the same ground was a mass of seething water. They knew the ice-cold water of the burn as it flowed over rock and the peaty taste higher on the hill. They knew the ecstatic stretch of body and rip of claws that tore deep satisfying scores in the bark of the trees. They knew comfort at night, curled close, their mother's fur against their heads, and the soothe of her tongue when a paw was hurt.

Not only the kits had grown. Owl and eagle and hawk had young that demanded more food than the adult bird required; the fox had half-grown ravening cubs; the rabbits were larger and those on the hill had survived by wile and guile, and were not so easy to catch, and the grouse chicks also had learned the laws of existence in the wild and were elusive, although when caught they provided a larger meal.

Chia no longer haunted Fergus's house for food. By day the old gander wandered and his quick senses told him of her presence. By night his warning call brought the keeper and his gun. The wildcat had only two chances to keep her line alive. She was not risking either the kits or herself.

Her lessons became stringent, demanding the kits' full attention. She showed them the safe places among the trees; how to dodge, and how to hide. How to melt into the shadows, formless, faceless, eyes narrowed to slits to prevent the light gleam, every muscle held taut, stiller than the stones that speckled the ground, ready to fight and slash and kill if hiding did not win the day.

They learned the sight and sound and smell of every beast that walked on the mountain, and knew hawk and owl, eagle and osprey; sparrow and chaffinch, grouse and capercaillie. Daily their senses became greater. They recognised the vibration in the ground when Fergus walked, so that he never glimpsed them, and as they left his birds alone and he knew that the eagle was taking the grouse, he thought that Chia must have lost all her kits and deserted his territory. Once he climbed above the eagle's eyrie, when both parents were absent, and looked down and saw the wildkit skeleton among the others that strewed the nesting site, so that he was aware that at least one kit had gone to feed the crouching fledgling that saw him and hid from imagined danger under uplifted sheltering wings.

The kits prospected every tree in their domain; knew how to climb swiftly and hide in dense leaves, or sprawl along a branch, invisible from below and unscented as the scent blew away on the wind. They knew the bramble thickets and the twisting paths that would take them into dense shelter, and they knew the noise that the wind made, keening into a gale, and the sound of the breeze whining softly over the grass on a summer day.

They knew the runs made by the mice among the grass stems, and Fury, drinking one dawn when the light was still grey and day as yet no more than a hint on the horizon, saw a small trout, and slapped it with clawed paw and caught it. He was astounded as the flapping creature landed on the bank, but killed it and enjoyed the taste, and after that, when mice were too clever and the rabbits had vanished, he became angler, and watched for the movement in the water, and rapidly increased his skill.

They knew the hides among tumbled rocks, the deserted den of a fox on the high part of the hill; the back entrance of an abandoned badger's earth on the shoulder of the glen; the dry overgrown run of a ditch, through which it was possible to steal unobserved and where it was safe to lie, scent masked by the massed smell of summer flowers that grew everywhere. This was only used in emergency as the strong flower smell worried the cats, drowning other scents, making it impossible to detect the rank tang of the fox or the delicate enticing smell of feathered prey.

There was less time for play. Hunting was difficult; birds flew off as the cats approached, the rabbits fled to the sanctuary of their burrows, the mice hid in holes and niches and evaded capture. All the foolish young had died. Now there were only those with wit and skill and cunning. The young hares were half-grown and fleet, knowing how to dodge and twist and turn and leap aside. All three cats were lean. Jade, slender and very small for her age, was capable of immense speed and her attacks were usually successful, when she found her prey. Fury lacked patience and sometimes pounced too soon, and suffered because Jade no longer shared with him, and nor did Chia, knowing her son must fend for himself.

Each night the wildcats hunted alone, within sound but not within sight of each other. By day they returned to lie curled close and warm, savouring company, but there were new emotions stirring in them. Fury felt the call of the wind and the call of something beyond himself, driving him to leave his mother and sister. Yet he was afraid to venture into the lonely wild beyond the land he knew, and risk unknown disasters.

One night when the moon was high and shadows danced over the ground, deceiving the kittens into thinking there was movement when there was none, Fury was so hungry that he went at dawn to find trout. There had been rain in the hills. Rain that fell from bleak skies that held enough water to burst the clouds, so that while he was fishing the burn began to rise. He caught two small fish and ate them and, his hunger appeased, when a third landed on the bank he did not kill it. He watched it flap and, amused, slapped at the twitching tail. The fish beat its body against the whiskered face and fell, and flapped again. Fury tapped it with a paw, concentration complete, caution forgotten.

A hungry stoat was questing for food near by. She had slipped her eel-like body into a rabbit warren, darting and diving along the narrow tunnels, her nose working busily. Nothing remained but a smell that provoked her already raging appetite to an agony of desire. She ached for food. There were fewer rabbits on the hill although myxomatosis, which had decimated the rest of the country, had not taken hold here. The beasts were isolated and the keepers had not seeded the land with dead, contaminated carcases. The living foxes, stoats, and eagles kept the rabbits from plaguing too widely.

Even so there were too many hunters prowling the hill. The stoat fared badly. She was young and had not yet borne a litter, although she had been ripe for a mate for two seasons past. She was chary and afraid of the males and ran from them. She slipped out of an empty burrow in a night of bright moon which flung barred shadows under the soughing trees. A wind sighed over the grasses and rustled the branches and tapped the leaves. It stroked her from nosetip to tailtip and she lifted her head eagerly and questioned its news.

News of birds near by. Out of reach, out of sight, but not out of scent. Her appetite sharpened, her lips were wet with saliva, her tongue slavered. Food was an urgent need. As yet she was not weakened by hunger, but weakness came fast when prey was scarce and the weak could not hunt or catch the victim they tracked.

She heard the slap of the fish on the bank. She ran, undulant, small clawed paws whispering over the ground, black-tipped tail alert, sharp-nosed, bright-eyed, eager. She saw Fury and she saw the fish. She did not see Chia, who was lying in the tree above the bank having emptied the nest of baby squirrels. The stoat paused. Chia hissed. Fury glanced up, saw the vicious fangs in the open mouth, and sprang to one side as the stoat tensed her muscles for the final dart that would break his back.

He sprang the wrong way. A moment later he was floundering and gasping in the icy water of the burn. The stoat, an agile swimmer, ran towards the bank, and Chia leaped from the tree and raced towards her.

Her quick pounce took her on to the stoat's back. The small head turned, vicious, seeking a death grip, but Chia had the advantage of weight and surprise and though the stoat twisted eel-like and bit deep, the would-be killer died. Chia left the body, looking for Fury, as she had seen him fall. Jade came and fed on unexpected bounty, while her mother raced along the bank, watching for her son.

There had been rain in the hills. The gathering clouds had built to thunderheads, the thunderheads had flashed viciousness in lightning forks across the sky, the rain had burst from them and flooded the ground, and trickles from the rocks had swollen and merged, and met in the the burn that ran peaty, foaming and fierce, between its banks, narrowly contained by them.

The water surged over rounded boulders that gave way against its force. White foam frothed along the bank, and the noise and din and tumble was deafening. Fury was battered and bruised. He sank and rose again to the surface, gasping, choking, never before having ventured deep. He struggled to swim, his paws working furiously, finding that he could keep his head up if he paddled frantically and used his legs to keep him afloat. He could do no more. The current thrust him along, tossed him sideways, flung him against rocks that protruded from the water, blinded him with spray.

Chia saw her son's head floating on the tumbling burn and followed it along the bank. She dared not jump in, knowing from past experience that the force of the water would not let her near. She watched him borne helplessly towards the waterfall.

There was a tree trunk jammed across the fall. The gap beneath it was sufficient to let water rush through so that a bridge was formed. Chia ran on to the slimed bark, her claws gripping tight, biting deep into the spongy surface. She waited, oblivious to everything but Fury.

He was exhausted, bruised, and battered, flung like drift-wood from side to side. His body was cut by rocks; his muscles ached; he was conscious of nothing but the need to keep alive. His frenzied paws worked furiously.

Chia subconsciously computed distance. She watched as the kitten came towards her, and as his small body was swept to the gap beneath the tree trunk, she sprawled, her paws, on either side, grappling for purchase, and her sudden darting head caught the kit's loose fur. Her teeth closed painfully and she arched herself, paws gripping the tree, muscles tensing, and lifted him to lie beside her. He was no longer a small kit but a half-grown cat, and before she lifted him the sweep and thrust of the current almost pulled her into the water, so that, briefly, her head was submerged.

She held him with her paw. He was panting, sickened, exhausted. He was bruised and battered and blood poured from several deep cuts. It was not safe on the tree trunk. He was weakened and might fall in the water. She dragged him along the tree. He was too exhausted to protest.

The wildcats lay together on the bank, gasping. Jade had eaten, and then followed her mother's trail. She came on the wildcat, now washing Fury, and she licked the blood from her brother's wounds, tending him gently. Chia washed her own face, and then returned to her son. The busy tongues soothed and warmed him. Blood welled from a deep cut on one shoulder and a gash scarred his forehead. One claw was almost dragged from its sheath. Saturated fur clung to his half-drowned body, which was extremely thin. The feeding had been poor for more than two weeks. Chia nudged him. They needed shelter. She was tired and Fury was vulnerable. He stood, and followed, limping painfully, unable to keep up with his mother and sister, so that they came back to him, to guard him, watching the shadows, knowing that the owl lurked and the fox might come and there were other stoats as well as polecats and weasels.

At the least sound Chia crouched and the kits froze, eyeing the land. Twice they stopped and identified a stag, snorting in its harbour. Once the shadow of a late-hunting owl glided across a clearing and somewhere in the dawning, a few minutes later, some creature died in an agony of squeaking. The rounded wings moved silently as the owl flew back to his young with his catch, a large brown rat dangling from the bird's beak, distorting his shadow. It was minutes before Chia hissed her kits to move again, and Fury limped after her with a painfully beating heart, knowing that if death dropped on him from the sky he had no strength to fight.

The badger's earth was too far away, but Chia knew of a small cairn close to a hollow tree that had died many years before. She led the kittens to it and looked inside, cautious, alert. There was the stale scent of a fox that had sheltered there days before, seeking a dry bed out of the rain. He had left the bones of a dead rabbit behind him and Jade played with the skull, tapping it so that it rolled. Chia licked Fury, washing him all over, her healing tongue soothing him, so that although he shivered with cold he relaxed tight muscles and his aching body rested. He slept.

His adventure was memory when he woke. He was dry, and he licked at his shoulder and washed his face with his paw. The cuts had scabbed but were sore. He was stiff and every muscle ached. Jade lay against him, her warm body a comfort, but Chia had gone. Fury gazed drowsily at the opening that led to the hill but he was too tired to follow or to look for her. He tucked his head under his paws and slept again and when Jade woke she washed her brother's cuts, and cuddled closer to him, as always needing company.

Chia was hungry too. They had fed thin in the past days, eating only a few small birds, and a rat, caught as he emerged from the burn, which he had swum after making a foray on Fergus's chicken sheds, looking for eggs. Chia did not want to hunt near man but she had little choice. She had chased a young rabbit the night before, but he was fleet and unafraid and entered a burrow which was too small for the wildcat. Jade, smaller and emboldened by hunger, followed him down, but he kicked loose earth in her face and she was forced to stop and wash away the pain in her eyes. She retreated, hungry.

Chia followed the deer trail that led to the hill above the keeper's house. The place was deserted and the gander walked on the edge of the tarn where the ducks swam. There were young ducks, more than half-grown, and Chia's mouth watered. Brilliant sunlight glittered on the water.

She lay in dense undergrowth, watching. Not a sign of man or his dogs. Fergus was on the sheep hill looking over the growing lambs. There had been a number of small ills among them, and two had died and the eagle had taken them. The keeper was far from home, busy with his own affairs.

Chia tasted the wind. It brought her news of the birds on the water; it told her of the hen houses; it was her guardian and her protector, giving no hint of her presence to the creatures below her. The gander did not hear her. He too was busy, engaged in hunting for food, his ears active, listening. He was untroubled. No sound betrayed the wildcat.

Sound and scent were her enemies. She crept downwards, her body flattened, close to the ground, feeling with sensitive pads for sticks that might snap and reveal her or leaves that might rustle. Paw-pad by paw-pad, inch by slow inch, whispering along the ground, breath held, eyes narrowed, every sense alert, she inched towards the edge of the water.

The tarn was small, one side of it thrusting towards her in a narrow inlet. Here a single duck dived for food, white tail twitching. Waiting was almost more than Chia could bear, but she did not allow her hunger to betray her. She glided, using every inch of cover, unheeded and unscented.

The wind was kind, blowing constant out of the South West, sleeking the fur along her back, informing her that she was near her goal, that food was beneath her, that triumph lay within her reach.

The bushes did not extend as far as the tarn. The last few feet were bare ground, untroubled by twig or leaf. The gander had his back to her. The duck was swimming towards the bank. He was unaware of danger and he waddled purposefully out of the water. Chia finished her stalk in a flash of movement, a spring, a twist, and a race for the security of dense undergrowth. Before the gander had time to shout his warning, she was back among the bushes, streaking for the den where the kits lay hidden, the duck dangling from her jaws, his short life ended.

The gander clamoured his warning; the other ducks quacked and huddled in fright, but there was no one to hear. That night when Fergus penned the birds he thought the fox must have come hunting and did not suspect Chia. He had almost forgotten her. She had been wise to leave his birds alone.

She came to the kits by a devious path, afraid of day. She knew that Fury would not be able to hunt for himself for some days, so that she shared with him. The three wildcats lay in deep bracken and divided the duck and the warm flesh gave them new strength. Fury was too exhausted to eat more than a few mouthfuls, but the meat helped restore him and, when he woke just before dusk, he fed heartily. At dusk he limped into the clearing but, when he had torn his claw, he had also strained his leg and movement was painful. He lay in the shelter of the brambles, savouring a rare warm wind that crept out of the South and he tasted the darkness which was full of scent. Flower-scent and tree-scent, bird-scent and beast-scent; roebuck guarding his family near by; sheltering hinds with calves at foot, a brooding stag, alone, lying deep in a bed of bracken, his antlers grown and soon to be cleaned and ready for the rut. Fury chewed the bones of the duck, and listened, sniffed, and waited, while Chia and Jade hunted.

They had small success. Only the fleetest and most cunning rabbits had survived the forays of the wildcats and the foxes, the owl, the hawk, and the eagle, and these knew better than to be caught. They sheltered in twisting burrows that were too narrow for the wildcats to follow, and their sentinels gave warning long before danger was near.

Only the swiftest birds now lived on the hill. The mice hid deep in narrow tunnels, out of reach of questing paws. Life was a hungry business. Chia caught a very young rat and shared it with Jade, but it made a small meal for the pair of them and there was nothing left for Fury.

Jade, hunting in a moony clearing, watching for the shadow of the owl, heard a rustle among the leaves. It might be mouse or perhaps a too-young chick, born late. She stalked the sound, curious. Chia was hunting along a track redolent of leveret, but the leveret was cunning and crossed a small burn and leaped sideways and she lost the scent. She returned to the clearing in time to see Jade thrust her paw to pat something that slid through the leaves. There was flash of movement and a hiss and Chia ran and sprang in a frantic movement that brought her on to the snake's back behind his wicked viperine head. She bit his neck. There was a twisting diamond-patterned wriggle and his body contorted uncannily for minutes after he died. Chia snarled at Jade, who stared at the snake. She had never seen such a beast before, but now she added it to her memory of hedgehog and shrew, as untouchable, although she did not know why. Neither did Chia. All that remained in her mind was the memory of her own mother killing a snake when Chia herself was a kit and had played with the wriggling tail that twisted temptingly on the ground. Her mother had slapped at Chia and slain the strange beast. Memory and instinct combined together.

That night Fury was left alone while Chia and Jade slipped over the hill, driven by the need for food. Chia called, her cry weird on the night, and Jade, hunting near by, answered. Fury heard the call. He had left the den, drawn by the sound of a mouse-tail sliding through the grasses. He killed swiftly and ate, and returned to the hollow, his leg aching. Jade hunted with her mother, watching for danger, and when she heard the whipwhoop of the owl she fled to shelter and found Fury already safe in hiding. The kits were larger now, but still feared the bird and they crouched and listened to the wind whining and the owl calling. Chia returned a few minutes later carrying a young hare.

Fury's lame leg healed. He hunted nightly, but the yield was small and he was hungry. Jade fared little better. Chia, having hunted for all of them for so long, was ravenous and she returned to the ducks on the tarn. She slipped down the wind and took one while Fergus was busy with the sheep. He, returning late and tired, swore, blaming the foxes.

Like the Labradors and the sheepdog, Jackie knew that the smell on the ground near the tarn was wildcat and not fox, but he could not tell the keeper. He was wary, unsure of the beast that had left such a trail. He knew foxes. He knew how they fought, how they could turn, and pounce, and bite. He could outwit them. This was strange. He sniffed through the rough ground, puzzled, and hunted in the bushes trying to find the source of the smell, but Fergus always recalled him long before he had tracked the wild beast down.

On the fourth day from Chia's killing the second duck, the kits followed her, knowing she had brought food which she had not shared with them. They chewed the bones she left and nosed the feathers. Fury had been driven almost mad by the smell of the bird and tried to take it from his mother. She slapped him with an armed paw, slashing his face, drawing blood. He stared at her and hissed in temper, but she did not change her mind. Her warning snarl drove him to the tree. Presently he joined his sister and hunted mice, but the smell of the duck was in his nose and mouth so that he salivated copiously, and he resented his mother's actions.

He did not lie with Chia and his sister that night but found himself another home near by, under the twisted roots of gnarled tree, on a drift of leaves, and he would not allow even Jade to share with him. Jade lay beside her mother. Chia licked her daughter's head, responding to the small beast's importunate pleas for affection.

When the wildcat woke she drank, and both kits followed her at a discreet distance. She ignored them and took the trail that led to the ducks on the tarn. Jade and Fury watched from the bracken bed. They noted how she stalked and caught and raced away just as the old gander called his angry warning. Again she took her catch and refused to share with them. The kits stalked in their turn, but each time the gander saw or heard them and each time his anger drove them to the trees, out of his reach as he ran, neck outstretched, berserk, chasing them off. Neither dared attack him. They knew his noise might bring the man and left the place, and went to sleep hungry.

Hunger stalked hourly beside them. Hunger made them careless so that they pounced too soon and lost their prey. Hunger sent them foraging into strange places. Hunger brought them among the sheep.

Chia made havoc among the ducks. Fergus had now lost three and his anger was sharpening. There was work to do among the sheep, but as soon as he found time he would lie in wait for the fox that was killing his birds. He penned them by day with the chickens. Chia lost her food source.

She followed the kits to the sheep hill. Here there were also deer and the air was ripe with the smell of prey. Lambs played beside their mothers, dancing and jumping on slender legs; the young deer were growing and played too, endless games of chase and tag which ended in exhaustion and a sudden dive for mother's udder and quick refreshment.

The mothers were wary. A bleating of sheep sent the flock huddling together and then speeding away, and brought Fergus to find the cause of the disturbance. The wildcats knew better than to show themselves. Fury crouched in the bracken, his tail curled round his feet, and watched. He noted everything. He knew that the man always came up the far trail; he knew the four dogs, though he did not appreciate the danger of the Jack Russell. He knew that he could no longer expect his mother to hunt for him.

On the third day of his vigil his patience was repaid. A ewe died. Fergus flung the body on the trail to take home to feed the dogs. Fury, finding it unattended, began to drag it into the bracken.

Jackie was running through the morning, alive and alert. He smelled cat and chased towards the smell and found Fury, his mouth full of sheep wool. Jackie barked and leaped at the wildcat. Fury let go of the carcase and twisted and ripped at the Jack Russell's shoulder. Jackie yelped and bit deep and the wildcat turned again and raked his paw across the terrier's face, narrowly missing the eye. Jackie held on grimly and the Labradors came running, Tim barking and Bran snarling as he snapped at the cat. Fergus heard the din and his heavy feet pounded over the ground, Rob racing after him.

Fury acknowledged defeat. He saw the gun. He might fight the dogs but he could not fight the man. He leaped away, racing for the trees, and climbed fast, leaving the grounded dogs leaping and barking. Pandemonium reigned on the hill as bird notes picked up terror calls and sheep ran blindly from unseen danger, bleating, and the deer stamped, barked, and fled. Fergus aimed, but the leaves grew thick and the wildcat leaped from one tree to the next, using its trunk to hide himself. Man and dogs hunted unavailingly for over half an hour and then the keeper picked up the dead ewe and took the trail home, whistling the dogs.

Fury remained in the tree until dusk brought the bats to flitter across the sky. He licked the deep bite in his shoulder and his sore paw. Jade and Chia had left him. He was quite alone.

CHAPTER ELEVEN

Fury watched a glitter of light on high cloud, saw the thin new moon slide out of hiding, and was intensely aware of the night-time secret dark. He knew that a stag sheltered near him. The smell of its warm body tickled his nostrils; he could also smell the sharp distinctive scent of crushed bracken, bruised and broken by the beast as he lay close, head stretched along the ground, brooding, half-sleeping, ears and nose alert. The faintest sigh of danger, the vibration of a thumping rabbit, the hollow call of an owl, all stirred him to watchfulness, as they stirred Fury, spread along the thick branch of a tree near by.

Chia's son was no longer a kitten. His body was more than half-grown, the rich fur streaked and striped and gleaming. He had learned much from his mother but he had much more to learn from experience. Until now he had relied on Chia and Jade's ears as well as his own to warn him of impending trouble. From this night he would often be alone, dependent on himself, wild, and wary. Later the urge to find a mate would dominate him and he would roam until his need was satisfied. Driving desire did not yet tease him. He was too young. He needed a place of his own, a hunting territory, but the thread that bound him to Chia was not yet broken. He did not wish to be alone.

At present hunger was paramount. Hunger broadened his nightly prowl, sent him questing uneasily on new paths, avoiding the open spaces that would reveal him to lurking hunters, though now he had little to fear from any but man.

He dropped from the tree. The stag heard him and turned a watchful head, but the stag was large and Fury did not wish to test his skill against such quarry. He skirted the clearing and ran down the hill, aware of wind on his fur, of damp ground underfoot, of the sighing rustle in the trees, of the far-away sea sounds, of the calling owl, and a sudden swift flurry that proved to be a hedgehog rooting for food. Fury gave the creature a wide berth. He needed food but he remembered the prickling spines.

Summer had sighed away and autumn coloured the trees. A moment later he heard the thrust of a heavy body among the new-fallen leaves. The old boar badger was hunting. He smelled the wildcat and ignored him. His interest centred on the hedgehog. Fury climbed a tree and watched, curious, as the badger lumbered towards the prickly beast. The spines were no protection from the boar's crushing teeth. Within minutes the creature was dead and skinned expertly. Fury smelled the kill. His hunger rose to a peak, dominating him, and he slid swiftly down the trunk and raced along the track that led to the rabbit hill.

There were no rabbits. Not a sign of white scut or bounding long-eared body. The wind had heralded his coming and every beast was safely hidden. Thwarted, his hunger sharpened by the rabbit smell that lay chokingly on the ground, Fury returned and skirted the clearing.

The badger had eaten and gone. The wildcat licked at the inverted hedgehog skin, but there was little nourishment left. Fury discarded it and hurried past the mouth of the badger's home, where freshly dug earth had been thrown in a heap, and the sow was busying herself bringing out the soiled bedding. The cubs played at tag under the moon. Fury watched them, his tongue licking avidly at his lips. The sow scented him and called, and in an instant the cubs were running pell-mell for sanctuary and their mother was chivvying them inside, her eyes glancing suspiciously about her. She smelled the wildcat but she could not see him.

Fury hunted, and fed on little creatures which never satisfied his hunger. He looked for his mother and sister but did not find them. The hill was noisy by day, the air constantly assaulted by the roar of rutting stags. The young wildcat could not understand the excitement that surged among the beasts nor the frequent clash of antlers as they vied for mastery. They chased him whenever he appeared, enraged and incautious. He left the hill, and found a den beneath a rocky cairn on the moor not far from the road. He was lonely, hungry, and forlorn.

Meanwhile Jade and Chia fared as badly, finding little to eat. They were thin. They were hungry. There was no time for play and the cold nights of autumn found them desperate for food.

Each day brought cunning to other creatures bred on the hill, ensuring that there were fewer of the unwise and unwary, the careless and the sick. They had to find new hunting grounds.

The manplace was temptation. Chickens and ducks scratched in the yard. Rats and mice haunted the barn. There were also scraps from the midden and an occasional bone taken outside by one of the dogs. There was danger, but not to those that watched in secret from the trees, learning his comings and goings and knowing his routine. Chia lay close and Jade lay beside her, and they waited their time.

Fury, ranging further and further from his birthplace, left the manplace alone and fed meagrely, but he fed. He did not trust the dogs nor the man whose activities were so extraordinary.

Fergus found another dead sheep with its skull picked clean and knew that this was wildcat and not fox trouble. He had more free time and he planned destruction. He changed his habits, and hid one night, leaving a window open and a lamp lighted, while he and the dogs crouched behind a low wall, watching. He checked the wind and waited, cold and cursing.

Tip, finding the open window, flew gaily outside to look for his master. Fergus did not see the bird. Tip alighted on the wall, glancing eagerly about him, and in that moment Jade, who had been prowling near, saw the flash of wings in the dusk and sprang. Tip died in a scream and a flurry of feathers and the Jack Russell ran, barking, towards the sounds. Fergus jumped up, furious. He had given no command. Jackie and Jade met above the pitiful fluff of feathers that was all that remained of Tip. The terrier drew immediate blood, and his teeth fastened to the young wildcat's shoulder. She, held in thrall by a ferocious demon, rolled and tried to bite at his neck, and her vicious hind claws ripped into his belly.

Fergus shouted, hoping the wildcat would run from man, but Jackie refused to let go. He held tight, his teeth gripping fiercely, and another vicious kick lashed his side, tearing through skin and muscle. Fergus fired at the air, hoping the shot would terrify the wildcat into flight. He dared not shoot at the intertwined bodies. Jade had no choice. She tried to free herself from the terrier; she screamed, hoping that Chia would come to her rescue, but Chia was hunting among the trees. Jade had come alone.

She had no chance. Tim came to help Jackie and the two dogs worried and ripped. Fergus tried again to call them off, afraid that the mother wildcat might come to the youngster's aid, but Chia was too far away.

Fergus watched the struggle. He was helpless and angry, and wished he had left the dogs indoors. He called Rob to heel. The sheepdog sat and watched, obedient, but whining his desire to join the fight. Blood poured from Jackie's wounds. Tim had a lacerated shoulder and a torn ear. A gash ripped across his face, narrowly missing one eye. The din of cat and dogs was astonishing, disturbing all the other animals. Kit and Katie lowed, the ducks quacked, the gander added his cackle, and higher on the hill the sheep were bleating, milling in panic, senseless and afraid. The deer raced for shelter, terrified. The hill was alive with fright and anger, and Chia crouched, wary, deep in cover, unable to identify the cause of the turmoil.

Jackie shifted his hold and bit deep into the wildcat's neck. His teeth tore her jugular vein. The fight was over. Fergus called the dogs, and looked down at the wildcat's torn body. She was far from grown. The mother cat must still be out on the hills, and perhaps her brothers and sisters too. He left her where she lay. He picked up the Jack Russell and also Tip's small body, which he took with him into the house. He had had the bird for more years than he could remember and would miss the sessions with Tip perched on the back of his armchair, tweaking mischievously at his hair. Later he would bury the dead jackdaw, denying the creatures that hunted the night the right to his body. He took the dog indoors.

He had to carry Jackie. The animal had no strength left.

He was lacerated and bitten, and breathless, and stared up at Fergus with anguished eyes. Fergus laid the Jack Russell gently on the rug and looked at him helplessly. He had hoped that most of the blood covering the dog had come from the wildcat, but now he saw that the little beast was mauled beyond recovery. He set his mouth grimly. He had an especial fondness for the Jack Russell. He stroked the terrier's head and Jackie wagged a feeble tail. The keeper inspected Tim. The Labrador had several bad gashes and two bites but he would survive. Bran, sheepish, came through the open door and looked at his master, but Fergus did not notice him, nor did he realise that the younger dog had cowered behind the wall, terrified by the noise of the fighting wildcat and dogs and by the clamour that deafened him. Bran was not usually a coward but he had seen nothing as vicious as the wildcat before.

Tim could wait. Fergus brought cloths and water, and began to bathe the Jack Russell's wounds, hoping his surmise was wrong, but as he worked he was forced to acknowledge that all hope was gone. The little dog could never survive his injuries. Days of pain lay ahead, followed inevitably by death. There was no choice. Fergus knelt on the hearthrug, swearing under his breath, his vocabulary extensive and vicious. He could not bear the terrier's pain-filled eyes or the knowledge of his next action. He poured himself a tot of whisky and drank it swiftly, and then gave milk and whisky to the little dog. Jackie could not drink. His throat was torn.

Fergus called the other dogs. He shut them in the gun-room, shaken by the silence. Tip always waited there and greeted his master raucously, wings flapping, voice cawing a delighted welcome.

The keeper returned, bleak-faced. He lifted the terrier gently, his voice soothing. It was difficult to speak. He took the little beast into the dawnbright garden, where the wind murmured in the trees and the grey light before day drained the world of colour.

The birds heralded dawn. The eagle was already aloft, his quick eyes watching the ground below him.

Fergus was aware of the sun rising red over the moor, of the whip of the wind on his face and its mournful keen in the bushes, of the dead body of the wildcat lying beyond the garden. He hated her, and hated her even more because of what he now must do. Jackie licked at the keeper's hand. The man's resolve was weakening, but the dog whimpered in paid and sudden terror, and there was no choice. There had been no choice from the moment that he had picked the little beast up from the ground where he lay above the inert body of his victim.

The sheepdog and the Labradors were whining as if they knew what was to come. Fergus swore again, relieving his feelings with vindictive expletives that brought no relief.

He fetched a gun, choosing the ·22 Remington automatic that he used for small game. He loaded it fully, not considering his action, loathing himself, the rifle, and his task. He went outside. Jackie was used to seeing his master with a gun and would not fear him. That almost made the deed worse. The sun was warming to autumn brilliance, to a rare hot day. The terrier saw the man returning and wagged his brief tail in feeble greeting. Fergus dared not greet or touch the dog. He dared not hesitate. He pressed the trigger and watched disbelief dawn in the brown eyes as the little beast twitched and died, relieved for ever of the suffering that would have been his had he survived.

There was not enough anger in the world to contain the hate that fired the keeper. He looked down at the dog, a lump in his throat. Poor dead Jackie, a brave little beast that had never known fear. He emptied his gun in futile spite, sending nineteen shots into the wildcat's dead body, and then took the carcase by the tail and flung it over the wall, to lie forlorn and undignified until the eagle salvaged it and soared into the sky. Gentle Jade was dead and, later, her mother returned and mourned her, quartering the ground where the young wildcat had died, knowing what had happened.

Fergus watched the eagle plunge and was briefly exultant, and then gloom returned. He brought Bran and Tim to see the dead terrier, knowing that if he did not they would wonder at his going and hunt the woods for him for days and never settle. They sniffed the dog's stiffening corpse, and lay, nose on paws, eyes sad, acknowledging death, and watched their master dig a deep hole in the soft ground of his kitchen garden and lie the Jack Russell there, stroking the bloodied fur, anguished by his betrayal of trust. He laid Tip in the grave. Perhaps in some other world the two would have one another for company. If only he had not had to deal the death blow himself. Yet there was no other way. In time his gun would end suffering for all the beasts that he took into his home, as it had ended it before for other well loved dogs and for badly injured sheep and Highland cattle.

Reason made no difference to Fergus's feelings. He marked the grave with a small post on which he wrote the dog's name, and added Tip's. There were five other graves, each one a memorial to some small animal that had graced his life briefly. A man lived too long, Fergus thought wearily as he went indoors.

He put down food for Rob and the Labradors, but they would not eat. He cooked himself a meal, and left the plate untouched. He made coffee, drinking cup after cup, and then summoned his energy and went to work with the sheep. He busied himself, filling his day, but no matter what he did or where he went he was haunted by the final disbelief in the small dog's eyes, by the fear that Jackie had had time to realise man's betrayal, and had died not understanding the mercy that prompted the deed.

When he went out, neither Labrador followed him. Fergus felt bereft, wondering if Tim and Bran, when they heard the shot, had guessed what had happened and were avoiding him, afraid in their turn of his betrayal of their trust.

Rob, as always, did his duty, but his tail was at halfmast and his manner subdued.

The morning was endless. The night, too, would have to be faced and Fergus feared sleep, sure that his dreams would punish him for his action. He bathed Tim's wounds. They would heal, though the slash across his face would scar the dog for the rest of his life.

The silence was daunting. Without Tip to tease him and without the dogs' busy prowlings and restless running and tail wagging the place was a desert. By lunchtime Fergus could stand no more. He persuaded himself that he needed the vet's opinion on Tim's injuries and put the chastened dogs in the Land-Rover and drove to the village, where for once he was glad to stop at the store and talk with the owner. Later he relaxed in the big kitchen at the vet's home and drank hot strong tea and ate griddle cakes, and watched as Tim's face was examined and dressed with a careful hand and the dog was given an injection. Tim did not falter. He waited, stoic, for the needle to pierce his skin. Bran, seeing the syringe, fled under the table, and Fergus was able to smile again, and able also to tell of the fight and of the end of his Jack Russell.

The vet and his wife listened without comment.

'I've been unlucky with terriers,' Fergus said regretfully. 'I lost Dougal...'

'Down a foxhole,' the vet said. 'They're brave little beasts. Too brave for their own good.'

He poured more tea and stoked the fire that kept the water hot and on which they cooked their meals. Flames shone small in the dog's eyes. The vet had put his own bitch outside. She was jealous of strangers. She whined and scratched at the door.

'I'd better be going,' Fergus said.

He whistled the dogs. The vet came to the door, knowing the keeper's thoughts.

'There's never any choice,' he said. 'Not at the end.'

It was poor comfort, and the words beat in Fergus's ears all the way home. That night he vowed vengeance. The wildcat was not rearing another litter on his ground. Jade had signed her mother's death sentence, and the tacit warfare that had been carried on intermittently during the long weeks since the kits were born was now a hunt to destruction, triggered by hate. The keeper needed revenge, and he needed to lay the ghost of two forlorn brown eyes that stared reproachfully before they glazed, losing all power of recognition. The wildcat's death might soften the memory of the little dog lying brutally mauled beside the toss of tumbled feathers that had once been Tip.

CHAPTER TWELVE

Chia had been hunting high on the hill when her quick ears heard the sound of fighting. She crouched, terrified, and then above the tumult she recognised Jade's voice. She ran towards the sound, arriving in the undergrowth within sight of the house in time to see the keeper stride to the dead body and empty his gun. Chia sorrowed bitterly. As soon as the man went indoors with the dogs she ran towards the garden, seeking cover to hide her. She found her daughter's mangled corpse. Then the man returned and she ducked into the bushes again, watching. She could not save Jade from the eagle now. When the Land-Rover drove away she returned and quartered the ground, desolate, mewing her anguish. Only Fury survived of the five kittens that she had borne, and she had not seen him for some days. She needed a safer home, away from the manplace, even though the hunting was easy and tempting. She went to look for Fury, but she could not find him. He had moved as far away from the man as he could.

Autumn tainted the air. The roar of the rut sounded on the hill. The dawns were chill and winter was coming. Chia needed a fresh food source and her ready wits told her where to find it, so that Fergus, hunting her all week, tracking with the dogs, found nothing. He discovered her lair and the tree where Fury had slept. The signs of the wildcats' claws, slashing the trunk, were plain to read. The keeper found dead shrews buried near. They were unearthed by Bran, who nosed them proudly but did not touch them, as dogs, too, hated shrewflesh. Fergus guessed that this was Chia's work and puzzled over them briefly. He knew that domestic cats never ate shrews although they killed them, as the flesh made them sick, and he wondered whether Chia, unable to resist a kill, had buried the body for the same reason or whether she had cached a food store, being, like the owl, immune. The number of untouched carcasses suggested that the wildcats never ate shrew, even when hungry.

The keeper tracked Chia from one lair to another but all were abandoned, and at the end of the week, he was forced to acknowledge defeat. She had outwitted him and he had not time to track her down. There was too much work to be done. For all that, he did not give up hope.

Fury was hunting on the moor. He had not seen Chia for several days, although he had looked for her. Now Chia too sought the moor. No other wildcat laired there and she looked for a place to lie. She found a crack in between a toss of boulders, the entrance thick with undergrowth, which would hide her from sight and shelter her from wind and rain. She lined her bed with leaves and dry grass and settled herself, brooding by day, lonely for her lost kittens. At night she hunted, savagery incarnate. She was wary and she was clever, and her instinct and her memory worked together to aid her.

The moor was bounded by the road that had been widened, that summer, to provide a connecting link for tourists between two major highways. Chia, watching from her new home, saw the speeding cars. She remembered the dead hare. She soon saw other things. Daily some creature died in a spill of blood or a flurry of feathers. The road edge, thick with stunted bushes and clumped twiggy heather and whinberry which smothered the thin-growing grass, gave the wildcat good cover and the road became her hunting ground. Between the infrequent vehicles, she raided the tarmac for its victims and took them to eat. It was a new kind of hunting requiring little effort. She found crow and pigeon, a young roebuck not yet old enough to carry antlers, and three times she found red deer and glutted herself. She did not need a daily hunt with such rich bounty. Once she found a slaughtered sheep.

Her quick ears heard the cars long before they drew near, and she flashed into cover so that no one saw her dragging the prey along the ground. With such ample food she recovered her strength. Her fur became glossy again, her eyes brilliant, and when she had fed she groomed herself meticulously, her busy tongue settling each hair in place and cleaning blood from jaw and whisker.

Nothing challenged her. When she had done, stoat and weasel and crow followed until the bones were clean. The smaller creatures she carried to her lair; the larger were eaten near the road. None of the travellers saw her nor guessed that she lay hidden, watching the sleek monsters speed by with a roar that ravished the silence. Only when sound had faded and become memory did she move from her hiding place.

With the return of energy came the return of speed. She prowled at dusk and dawn, haunting the glen, where small rustles marred the silence. There was the chitter of the racing brook that tumbled over rounded boulders, snaking through the trees, reflecting light in a glitter and dazzle that was never still. The birds told one another of her presence, so that her way was noisy with hatecall and fearcall, with the yak and cackle of danger.

Chia was aware of the birds but she did not hunger for them. The road provided her with constant bounty. She learned this strange territory slowly, always cautious, watching for man, her only real enemy. Man and the dogs that shadowed his heels. The criss-cross tracks led along ways beaten out by generations of deer, and deer-scent dominated all other scents. Here the big stags agitated, mastered by the exultation of the rut; here the hind herds guarded the year's youngsters, and their sharp alarm barks and sudden stamps were frequent.

Chia, lying full-fed and drowsy in a bracken patch, the sun hot on her fur, watched the young deer play and fight in mock battle. She was better fed than she had ever been in her life and with less effort. At times she was playful and tapped thoughtfully at a trail of grass, or stalked a dancing leaf. Then memory of her staid and sober matronhood came to her and she curled to rest. She made her nest inside the rocks deeper, using leaves and wool caught on the deer fence, and her bed was dry and sheltered from rain and wind.

She needed to remember every inch of ground so that she could run from danger. Some of the ground was new territory. She wandered, apparently aimless but in fact intent on learning every ridge and hollow, every bush and tree trunk, every cranny where she might hide in emergency.

Some days before winter chilled the land she found nothing on the road, although she patrolled for a greater distance. She returned, hungry. A small tarn lay among the grasses on the way to her home. Here a heron was fishing. He was standing, statuesque, beak poised, intent on the water. A fish darted. The beak lunged and the fish vanished. The bird moved ponderously, its long legs ungainly, its body humped against the sky.

Chia watched the bird, nose and tail twitching. Excitement mastered her. She could smell the birdsmell and knew that here was food. She crept forward, angling so that the wind would aid her, leaving her unseen. The grasses, spiky and coarse, were long enough to hide her. She parted them with her body, patient, ruthless, padding softly, her passage ghostlike.

The heron was absorbed. Fish were not plentiful in the tarn and he was hungry. Most of those he caught were fingerlings, a taste, a mouthful, a brief memory, rousing hunger rather than sating it. He was aware of the wind sliding over the grass tops and ruffling the tarn's bright surface, mirroring the dawn. He was aware of the water lapping his legs, of the soft suck of mud between the pebbles, of the glimmer of a fish darting in the shallows, and the silver glisten as he lifted it from the water, struggling to get away from the astonishing creature that towered above it.

Stand and watch and strike and feed, aware of sun strengthening to day, warming the feathers on his back. Chia watched. The long beak slashed the water. Chia sprang. She landed on the heron's back, her claws ripping, and her impetus carried both bird and beast into the reedy tarn. Chia did not let go. The wicked beak flashed towards her but she evaded it, and her teeth met in the bird's neck. She dragged the sodden mass of feathers to the bank, and crouched to feed.

There was a sound behind her. Her quick ears heard it and she turned swiftly, mouth open, snarling. Fury ran out of the grass. He had fared badly, never killing as much as he needed and he was hungry. He had heard the screech as the heron died. He was not sure of a welcome from Chia, but the wildcat remembered her son and greeted him with a swift mew of pleasure. He ran forward and they met nose to nose and moments later, the ceremony of greeting ended, they shared the kill.

They returned to the moor and hid beneath the tumble of rock that Chia had found, and were glad of one another's company. Chia washed her son and he purred loudly.

They hunted together. Chia showed him the bounty that lay on the road and, though at first terrified, he was ravenous and soon learned to snatch the dead that the cars had murdered. It was temptingly easy. It led to trouble.

Early one morning a young hind tried to cross the road to reach the trees new-planted by the foresters on the other side. She was hungry for young green shoots and wanted shelter from the wind that was now gusting to winter. The madness of the rut was ended and she had strayed from the herd. She bounded lightly, but she had never seen a road before and did not associate the unknown object that sped towards her with danger, nor could she judge its speed. It took her and tossed her, and she fell at the road edge, away from the moor. Chia had never crossed the road. She did not trust the roaring monsters that hurtled from nowhere, speeding towards her faster than the eagle dropping from the sky. Hidden in the bushes, she saw death overtake all the creatures that trespassed on the tarmac. She herself never ventured far and chose easy prey, lying close to the road-edge, that could be dragged swiftly into the bushes.

Fury, who had not fed well and was hungry, saw the deer die. He ran towards it, so intent on his victim that he did not hear Chia's warning snarl. A sports car, exceeding every speed limit, the driver entranced by the emptiness of the road in front of him, was upon the young wildcat before he had time to do more than turn his head in fear. The car ran straight over him and drove on. Chia crouched by the road-side, terrified.

The wheels had missed the wildcat. His shoulder was torn by the silencer, he was bruised and battered and bleeding but he was alive. He crawled to the edge of the wood. Chia listened. The air was still. Trembling, she raced lightly across the danger zone, her heart beating wildly. She ran to her son and licked at his injuries. He mewed plaintively. He was too battered to move far. He crawled to the edge of the trees, looking for cover.

Chia left him and pulled the deer from the road. She fed briefly and returned to Fury who lay quiet, limp, and shocked and sleepy.

The wildcat curled herself against him, her ears fanned, listening. They were unprotected from wind and weather, though the bushes hid them from sight. Two hawks were feeding on the deer. She watched through the leaves but she did not move, and when Fury eased his aching body and mewed forlornly her tongue was swift to reassure him and he was warmed by her presence and comforted by her company.

That night he was strong enough to crawl, very slowly, seeking better shelter. He was unable to fight or defend himself against an enemy, and even a prowling fox, knowing him to be injured, might well attempt to kill. Movement was agony, an aching and a tearing of severely injured muscles, and the wildcats were forced to stop while Fury rested, panting.

They found protection in the lee of a tiny cave, its entrance sheltered from the prevailing wind. Rain was drifting through the trees from a sullen sky that threatened a deluge later in the night. Chia hunted briefly and brought her son a young rabbit that had waited too long before he ran. Fury could not eat. He licked at the torn flesh and presently he slept again, and Chia fed herself and went to drink.

By morning Fury was too stiff to walk. His leg ached and his shoulder was swollen. Rain had collected in a tiny pool outside the cave and he dragged himself to the water to still his raging thirst. Rain fell all day, so that he could drink without effort, and that night he was able to eat some of the mouse that Chia brought to him.

She did not like the new territory. She longed for familiar places, uneasy because here she did not know where the weasel hid, or the polecat, or the fox and she was afraid. There were too many strange noises. The sound of cars was now familiar, but a puttering tractor sent her headlong into cover, trembling with fear. Later she and Fury listened, crouched in their hiding place, and the swelling song of the horn of a sports car, overtaking a grinding lorry, kept both wildcats safe in their retreat. They did not dare emerge for several hours.

By the end of the week Fury was able to walk again but he was slow, his injured leg paining him, and his pounce was mis-timed. Chia hunted for both but hunting was difficult. There was little life in the pinewood where they now lay by day, and she dared not try for the game that lay on the road. Both wildcats were very thin.

On the seventh night a pine marten slipped down a tree, leaving its nest, and sat in a clearing cleaning its face. Chia was watching deep in the shadows against a tree trunk. She slid on soft paws, approaching from behind and the marten never knew what had hit him. Chia took the body to Fury and they fed so well that they were able to rest for two days before they hungered again. They basked in the faint November sun, and Chia watched for both of them, and the warmth eased the soreness and stiffness so that when evening came Fury stalked and killed three mice.

Chia was homesick for her old haunts. She was uneasy, disliking new territory and though man dominated her old home she was forced to return. The place haunted her. That night she and Fury cautiously crossed the road and followed the track that led to the hill. Here they paused briefly to hunt rabbit. Chia found a young hare and chased and killed. By daybreak they were back in the lair that overlooked Fergus's house. It was impossible to leave familiar ground.

They had learned much. Neither wished to hunt in the farmyard nor to tempt the dogs. They avoided the man-place, though Fury was curious and watched the keeper, unseen, puzzled by the strange things that he did, by the tools that he used, by the spade that he carried and the pail.

They hunted high, watched by the eagle and his mate and the young eagle now spreading its own wings.

The keeper forgot them. They had not troubled him and he thought his war had ended and that all the wildcats were dead. He went about his business, unconscious of the eyes that watched him from tree or bush or lair, although the dogs knew they were there and often tried to tell him.

Beyond the house, Chia and Fury drifted ghostlike after their prey. Winter came early, bringing starvation as snow fell and ice covered the pond. One morning, tempted beyond endurance Chia descended swiftly, leaving her tracks plain to see, and snatched a duck that had been frozen in the water.

Fergus took the dogs and followed her trail to the lair on the hill. He knew that the wildcats were deep inside. There were two sets of tracks in the snow. He remembered his terrier and he remembered Jade. Above him the eagle watched, aware of the man and the dogs and aware of the gun. Chia and Fury lay in deep shelter. Fergus returned home.

He now knew where the wildcats laired and memory of his lost dog teased him so that while he finished the day's chores, and penned the farmyard birds, and battled with the snow, he whipped his anger. The brutes would hunt again in the yard while the snow lay thick. They would come to plague the lambs in the spring; there would be young born again on the hill and while they were growing the queen would feed fat and hunt for all of them. It was not to be.

That night he crept from the house and circled the trees. He left the dogs at home. There was light enough to see. The snow masked all sound, but he had to watch where he trod, lest he slip into a hollow or fall and break a leg.

He crouched above the lair, watching. Cold numbed his fingers. Cold chilled his ears until they ached. A harrying owl flew by and new flakes fell from the night. The cats emerged from the hole.

Sound was their ally but the night was still. Nothing moved. There was no stir to warn them of doom above them, watching for them, intending to kill. No scent to nudge them into instant retreat, no faint breeze to tell them that an enemy lay hidden near.

Fury had never seen snow. He sniffed at it, patted at it with his paw, and then pounced, landing in a playful flurry as the moon revealingly flung a glisten over the wood.

Fergus was spellbound, gazing at total beauty. The white

snow glimmered, the masked trees were hung with splendour, twig and branch, bough and trunk, grass and bramble, fern and heather tump, were remote from reality, and far below him ice glittered on the tarn and his own home was a palace, transformed and ethereal.

The two wildcats were chasing each other, alive, alert, entranced by the new dimension that had come to their world. They had no feeling of fear, no hint of imminent danger and as they chased through the trees, and stopped and patted at the snow, and hit out at the branches, and watched the small cascades slide to the ground, Fergus lowered his gun.

He could not shoot. He could not defile the snow with blood, nor bring death to the bounding graceful feline creatures that welcome winter and delighted in life.

The hill moved, as the wildcats played, and the soft mounds in front of him rose and revealed themselves as deer which had been masked as they slept.

They had sensed the cats and their elegant bodies shed the snow as they bounded gracefully downhill. The wildcats paused to watch. Chia nosed Fury. Fergus sneezed. A moment later the hill was quiet, and the only trace of the beasts that had played there was the scuffled trails that marred the deep unbroken white expanse, and a memory of beauty.

Fergus unloaded his gun lest he trip on his return journey. Snow was falling again, hiding the world. The light of his house glowed warm, beckoning home. It was good to find shelter, to shut out the cold, to enjoy a rare tot of whisky by the blazing fire, legs stretched to the welcome heat, while the dogs lay at his feet, dreaming, and twitching in their dreams.

He went upstairs and looked out of the window at the hill. He grinned, mocking himself for softness, but he was glad that he had not shot even though he had an easy and unusual target. The beasts were beautiful and they were rare. There were always predators. A man needed war and if he killed the cats he would have nothing left to hate. Tonight there was truce between them. Had he killed them he would have hated himself, and he could not live with that. He whistled the dogs and went to bed.

Outside, on the mountain, unaware of their reprieve, Chia and Fury hunted, and later curled together for warmth in their lair, and the winds of winter whined over the hill as the snow glittered under the gaze of the moon, and fear was leashed for the night.

CASEY
by JOYCE STRANGER

The touching story of a cat with a difference.

Life at Wayman's Corner could never be dull. Crises lurked around every corner... marital friction, careless city visitors, farmyard accidents, and Casey.

Casey, son of a Siamese tomcat and a black farmcat, was an animal with great determination, strong affections, and a nose for mischief, whose strange friendship with Sultan, the terrifying Jersey bull, becomes a central part of life on the farm . . .

0 552 08394 1 – £1.50

KYM
by JOYCE STRANGER

Joyce Stranger's novels have become well-loved favourites with all age groups. Her first non-fiction book is sure to take its place among them.

Kym is the autobiography of her Siamese cat who, for thirteen years, adored her, dominated her, and played havoc with her life. A more accident-prone cat never lived. Even on holiday he managed to turn their caravan into an ambulance or a peep-show. A born eccentric and voluble talker, a cat with the grace of a dancer and the instincts of a prizefighter.

An endearing story of the misadventures of a unique pet, seen through Kym's blue-eyed squint, and his owner's humorous and observant eyes.

0 552 10695 X – £1.50

JOYCE STRANGER NOVELS AVAILABLE
IN CORGI PAPERBACK

WHILE EVERY EFFORT IS MADE TO KEEP PRICES LOW, IT IS SOMETIMES NECESSARY TO INCREASE PRICES AT SHORT NOTICE. CORGI BOOKS RESERVE THE RIGHT TO SHOW NEW RETAIL PRICES ON COVERS WHICH MAY DIFFER FROM THOSE PREVIOUSLY ADVERTISED IN THE TEXT OR ELSEWHERE.

THE PRICES SHOWN BELOW WERE CORRECT AT THE TIME OF GOING TO PRESS (APRIL '83).

All these books are available at your book shop or newsagent, or can be ordered direct from the publisher. Just tick the titles you want and fill in the form below.

CORGI BOOKS, Cash Sales Department, P.O. Box 11, Falmouth, Cornwall.

Please send cheque or postal order, no currency.

Please allow cost of book(s) plus the following for postage and packing:

U.K. Customers—Allow 45p for the first book, 20p for the second book and 14p for each additional book ordered, to a maximum charge of £1.63.

B.F.P.O. and Eire—Allow 45p for the first book, 20p for the second book plus 14p per copy for the next 7 books, thereafter 8p per book.

Overseas Customers—Allow 75p for the first book and 21p per copy for each additional book.

NAME (Block Letters) ....

ADDRESS ....

....